WINTER

ANA CALIN

LORD OF WINTER

FAE OF DARKNESS

ANA CALIN

Table of Contents

CHAPTER I

Arielle

THE MOMENT I STEP INTO the Alpha Sigma fraternity house, I have second thoughts. The place is packed with boisterous football players coming on to tipsy girls, a couple getting it on right next to the main door. I try to back out, but my client Jasmine grips my arm, dragging me in.

"There he is," she says in my ear, pointing not very discreetly at a guy in the main room. He leans with his elbow on the mantelpiece, acting all seductive to a girl so drunk that she's reeling.

"The campus golden boy or what?" I say under my breath. "I don't know, Jazz. He doesn't seem right for you."

"It's who I want, and that's that." She creases her tiny nose, trying to look the boss. But she actually reminds me of a Tinker Bell illustration from a Peter Pan book. Even her dyed pink hair suits the vibe.

"Things aren't that simple."

"I'm paying you good money, aren't I?"

"Which is exactly why I should be completely honest with you."

"Oh, so generous of you."

"Jazz, don't you want to be with a guy who's truly head over heels for you, one who desires you, who genuinely—"

"Don't give me that bullshit, Arielle, 'cause I won't take it, not from you. You were a fucking prom queen, you can have any guy you want. Look at you." She motions to my body that's wrapped in a black wool dress that doesn't manage to hide my curves as much as I'd like. "The body of a mermaid, and the face of a Disney princess."

"Jazz—" I want to tell her it's not like that, that I've had my share of unrequited loves, that no one is exempt from that no matter their looks, but she won't have it.

"Just drop it, and do what I'm paying you to do."

"No, not until I'm sure that you fully understand what that involves." I straighten my back, taking advantage of the fact that I'm taller than her, considerably so in my high heels. I've got my hair tied in a strict bun, and my eyebrows are naturally highly arched, which should add to my air of authority. "What I'm doing will make him crazy about you for a few weeks, but the effect *will* wear off eventually. If he's not genuinely attracted to you, what you have won't last." I look at him and the girl by the mantelpiece. "You're not his type, and sooner or later he will return to, well, to *that*."

5

"It worked for my roommate," Jasmine insists with hunger in her eyes. "She's been with the guy ever since you cast your spell, I want what they have."

"That was different, he was already interested in her, but just too much of a chicken to make a move. My magic, it just nudged him, that's all." I place my hands gently on her shoulders that feel tiny under the leather jacket. "Listen, I don't want to lie to you. If there isn't some underlying attraction there, my magic will only spark a few days of crazy lust, that's all. Then the effect will gradually wear off, and he'll be left scratching his head and wondering what he saw in you in the first place. And that will hurt like hell, believe me."

She grips my wrists.

"I'll take him in whatever form I can have him, Arielle. Please."

I search her eyes, realizing just how deeply she wants this. I can read the hope in her eyes that she'll get the guy to genuinely fall for her in those few days of closeness. It's just self-delusion, and I know it, but she won't have it any other way. I decide on one last try to make her change her mind.

"You have a little brother, Jazz, imagine if someone were to do something like this to him. A girl using magic to manipulate his behavior."

"You're stalling," she growls. "Do it already."

I breathe in deeply. Okay, here it goes. I pull Jasmine in a corner of the busy main room. I went for the black wool dress and the tight bun with reason, namely that it helps stay more or less under the radar. Usually my half-fae appearance draws attention,

6

mostly because of the unusual clearness of the skin, and the shine of my hair. My eyes don't glow quite like a fae's, but still more than a human's, and I can't always blame it on the lighting. Which is why I'm wearing glasses with a thick, black rim.

I focus my attention on the boy by the mantelpiece. Aunt Miriam's words keep spinning in my head, the words she repeats to me every time I leave the house on a gig like this.

"You should stop using your magic once and for all." Her old crinkled eyes would deepen with worry. *"It's forbidden for fae and half fae to live in the mortal realm, let alone use their powers. We have to keep a low profile, if we want to survive."*

Not to mention that it's beyond forbidden to use our powers in order to help humans, and even more so for money. But I don't have much choice. Aunt Miriam wanted me to go to college, and that means I'm amassing student debt with every breath I take. I won't let her work herself to death in a women's prison to pay off my studies, just because she wants me to graduate like a human, and have a chance at a normal life.

"You need an actual career," she said. *"You won't be winning your bread with magic, or if you do, it won't be long until the Council of the Arcane gets hold of you, and throws you into the pit."*

Besides, she argued, we're not even witches to render magic services, but half fae. Our magic is different, we don't need Voodoo dolls, worms or lamb entrails, even though we could use them, if we wanted to. But that's beneath us. We're superior to witches, she says.

I focus on the guy, and connect my mind to the lake behind the house. I open my pores to feel the magic of water, and become one with it. As a half fae of water, water is what feeds my powers, along with the full moon, and the night. I can act much like a mermaid that sings and lures men to her, driving them insane with yearning, but I don't use my voice on gigs like this. The guys could actually lose their minds. So all I do is drive my magic into the guy's blood, drawing his attention like a magnet towards us.

I can feel Jasmine's hand clench around my arm, her blood pumping when his bad boy eyes rest on her. My magic ripples through him as he falls in love with Jasmine.

My eyes flutter, about to shut as I seal the deal quite literally with his blood, but the sound of thunder tears through the house, making the walls shake. I snap to attention just as lightning flashes through the large windows. The blood freezes inside me.

A hooded figure stands in the middle of the room. He just popped up out of nowhere. I squint at it. It's a man, a large one. I focus on his face, and my breath catches—he's fae. Even though this is the first time I've laid eyes on one since Aunt Miriam last showed her fae face, there's no mistaking the perfectly smooth skin, and the brightness of the eyes. Aunt Miriam has been wearing the disguise of an old woman for so long that I barely remember her features besides the perfectly straight ebony hair identical to mine, and maybe the strict shape of her mouth, but I remember the impact.

The fae man stares straight at me. Under his magic, time seems to have slowed down so much that nobody moves. But then I realize he must have frozen them all, since ice flowers spread over everything around him. He emits coldness. People are slowly turning into statues of ice.

The magic of water that was rippling under my skin turns to chills. Aunt Miriam used to tell me stories about the winter fae, a highly dangerous kind. They rarely ever cross the boundaries into the mortal realm, and when they do, it's always in order to punish wayward supernaturals.

Like me.

The fae is watching me out of dangerous eyes. His skin is so hard it glistens like wet stone, and the sharp contours of his face show that he's used to violence. A hood covers his head, and his cape hangs from unusually broad shoulders. He heads to me slowly, the wooden floor creaking under his heavy steps.

"Arielle de Saelaria." His voice is low like rumbling thunder, I can feel it vibrate between my ribs. "You are charged with high treason against the Council of the Arcane."

I should say something, but I can't even move my lips. All I can do is stare at him as he walks closer.

"You've been using magic for money, placing fae powers in the service of humans." Ice spreads over the walls as he speaks, creeping over the ceiling. The temperature dropped so much I'm afraid one touch would be enough to make the frozen humans explode into shards. Who the hell is this guy, some kind of executioner?

Speak, defend yourself, I scream on the inside, but I can't get my tongue to unstick from my palate. My body is frozen under his power. I want to look down at myself, but discover I can't move anything except my eyeballs. Thick strings of ice crawl up my body, the fae's ice magic chaining me from ankles to shoulders, hands behind my back. An icy feeling runs over my chest like an ice cube pressed against my bare skin, the cold piercing through my wool dress and the lace underwear underneath.

"Please," I manage faintly through cracking lips. "Let me, let me—" But even my thoughts freeze inside my head.

"You knew what you were doing, half fae," he says, now close enough that I can see his face clearly. "You can't blame this on lack of knowledge. You have deliberately misused fae powers."

A strand of hair as bright as gold falls from under his hood. He seems a vision straight out of a 3D fantasy movie, and if I wasn't frozen solid, I'd probably react somehow. His face seems sculpted in ice, and the strand of hair falling over his forehead makes me think of liquid gold. I have a strange urge to reach out and touch it, feel the fluid silk of it on my finger, but I can't freaking move.

He winds an arm around me that feels like a block of ice under his garment. He flexes just a little, but it's enough to throw me over his shoulder. I should try to scream and kick, but he's definitely larger than any human man could naturally be, and I'm worried about the consequences of antagonizing him. A beast on steroids must be hiding underneath his cloak.

With me over his shoulder, he moves so fast things speed by in a blur. The fraternity house loses itself in the distance, looking like it's been gripped in tentacles of snow, like an island of winter among the other houses.

How come there's no one out in the streets, no one to witness all this? I'm aware the fae must have frozen time along with the place, it's a correlation that Aunt Miriam told me about, but the other houses stayed untouched by snow. Must be his magic, he must have cast the fog of confusion over the humans' minds. By the time they'll come back to themselves, there will be little evidence left of all this.

The image warps, and disappears in a whirling spiral, like a centrifuge. My brain scrambles inside my skull, and I'm about to lose consciousness. My last coherent thought is that he must have plunged with me inside a portal between realms.

Arielle

THE SOUND OF DRIPPING water wakes me up. I open my eyelids slowly, but they're so heavy that it's a struggle. But the sound of water promises healing. I need to feel the power of water inside of me again in order to regain my strength.

I manage to lift my head from the cold ground. It smells rancid in here, and it's cold as fuck, snowflakes covering me. Things start coming back—the fraternity house, Jasmine, my magic on her crush, the fae man.

"Hey, you're alive," someone whispers.

I try to move my head in the direction it comes from, but a sharp pain stabs me in the nape of my neck.

"Help me, please." Damn it, my lips hurt with every word. They're deeply cracked, licking them I can taste the blood that has frozen to them.

There's a shuffle in the darkness. I strain to focus my vision, but it's blurred from the snowflakes clinging to my lashes. It takes a few moments of blinking to clear my eyes, and make out a pale heart-shaped face framed by white hair.

But the face looking at me isn't that of an old person. It's a girl with dirty cheeks, dressed in rags. She's clearly fae, with big beautiful brown eyes that sparkle with a lively spirit. Yet her eyes are the only thing that seems alive about her.

"I hear you used your magic in the mortal realm. Poor thing. They won't go easy on you for that."

"Please, help me."

She draws closer, looking down at my body to assess the state I'm in.

"I can't, you're wrapped in winter magic," she says.

"But you're a winter fae, aren't you? Your white hair... It emits cold, like snow. You must be able to do *something*."

"I am a winter fae, but a much lesser one than the man who wrapped you in these magic winter chains. I have nothing on that kind of magic."

I tense my chained body in such a way that I can look around, even if I can only pull off a few basic moves.

Jesus Christ, this is a dungeon. Frosty stone walls, emitting a chill that permeates my flesh and my bones. The bridge of my nose hurts from it, and my breath turns to steam in the air. As for my body, it's wrapped in what looks like thorny vines of ice, the thorns tearing through my wool dress and my black stockings.

My skin is so white from the cold, I resemble a corpse from the morgue. Aunt Miriam used to call me Snow White back when I was a kid because of my skin that was naturally white as milk, and contrasted with my ebony hair, but this is a whole new level of white.

"Oh, God, I'm going to die."

"That's it, despair," the girl says. "That will get your blood pumping, and heat you up."

"How can you stay so freakin' calm," I screech at her. "We're both in a dungeon, a frozen cell that's making us sick." I look at my bound body again, trying to check for wounds. "Not to mention that if we get wounded it'll draw rats and other creatures." I cringe as I imagine it, but the girl lets out a crystalline laugh.

"There are no rats in here, doll, it's too fucking cold."

"All right, all right, don't panic," I tell myself, looking around as much as my stiff neck allows, and trying to pull myself together. "There's got to be a reasonable way out of this." It hits me. "The man, the fae who brought me here. If I could just talk to him, explain. He took me because of the magic, I know he did, but if I told him—'"

The girl laughs and shakes her head like I'm an innocent child.

"Oh, you'd try to reason with him, yes? You're funny. No one will listen to anything you have to say, doll. If you're here, it's because you used magic in the mortal world." She motions to the grates. "Like many other prisoners here. That's an unforgiveable offense, no matter the reasons that prompted it."

"There are more people in here?" I whisper, my breath misting the air.

"Fewer than there used to be, but yes. The dungeons were once full of wayward fae, shifters, vampires, and even witches who actually used their skills for financial benefit." She leans over a bit like she's letting me in on a secret. "It's okay to trick people, you see, take their money like a charlatan, but not to actually use your magic to their benefit. Anyways, the Wards showed that they meant business by sending most of the wrongdoers to burn in the pit for tens of years, so not many supernaturals dare to go against the rules anymore."

"Are you saying they're going to burn me for this?" I don't know if I'm scared or just plain enraged. "For having cast a few spells, and helped a few girls with a crush?"

She shrugs. "They burned others for less, like influencing crops to grow faster. But there is hope, look at me. I'm still here."

"That's no surprise. You're only a child. They're just teaching you a lesson, for sure."

"A child, oh, wow, thanks for the compliment. But I'm a full-blood fae, that's why I look so young to you. You're used to humans, and their aging, and it's understandable that you're confused. But I've been around for a few good decades already."

Decades isn't old for a fae, I know that much from Aunt Miriam. I smile. "So you're around sixteen, only that in fae years. How long have they been keeping you here?"

"A few months, I think." She purses her lips, tapping them with her filthy finger as if she's not so sure anymore. "Could be a year or so."

"What in the world did you do to deserve this?" I can hardly still contain my rage. Now that I realize she's basically a teenager, it's making my stomach churn.

"Crossing into the mortal world, and going to parties. Humans may live the lifespans of ants, but don't they get all the fun." She smiles widely as she reminisces, her pretty brown eyes sparkling with fond memories.

"Parties? If that's what they're keeping you locked up for, they'll surely behead me."

"Well, as a fae I did draw some serious attention."

I let her talk, and tell me about her adventure in the mortal world; it helps me stay awake, not lose my consciousness again. I manage to crawl into a proper sitting position with my back against the wall, but the magic wrapped around me feels like a frozen cocoon, and I'm stiff all over. My eyelids fall heavy, it's a struggle to keep them open.

"Don't fall asleep," the girl urges, planting small slaps on my face. My cheeks are so cold that her fingers actually feel warm. "You'll fall into a coma, and it'll be hell to recover from it. Trust me, I've seen it before."

"Keep talking to me," I plead faintly. "What's your name, tell me about yourself."

"I'm Edith. Edith Snowstorm, born and raised in the Winter Realm. We moved to the Flipside a few years ago—you know, the mirror version of the mortal reality, the one inhabited by supernaturals."

"Yes, I know what the Flipside is."

"What exactly do you know?" she provokes when my voice comes out too faint.

"I'm so tired," I whisper. "I want to sleep."

"No sleeping." She slaps me hard, and I gasp, my back stiffening, icy thorns piercing me.

"You've got a heavy hand for a kid."

"I told you, I'm not a kid. Now tell me what you know about the Flipside."

"Like you said." I lick my cracked lips, the salt in my saliva stinging like hell, and kick-starting my brain. "The mirror reality. It's like the shadow version of the Earth, where the world functions by the rules of magic. Humans aren't allowed to cross into the Flipside, just as supernaturals are forbidden from crossing over into the mortal world. How did you manage to cross over, by the way? Portals are hard to find, only few humans ever did."

She slumps against the wall by my side, obviously relieved that I'm back. "It's easy to find portals for supernaturals. The Flipside is the closest realm to the mortal world, and crossing from one realm into the other can happen relatively easily for someone with magical powers. And I couldn't resist the temptation. I discovered I could cross over without much effort, and you know how it is—if you can, you do.

"So I made a friend, fulfilled her three wishes like a fairy from bedtime stories, and earned myself her unbroken loyalty. She took me along, showed me her world." She sighs. "Ah, the parties, the boys, the pot, I loved every minute of it."

"How could that life compare to the magic life of a fae?" I manage. "I craved the fae world all my life—only not like this."

I look around at our dreary surroundings. A freezing dungeon, where even the cockroaches died of cold, lying on their backs with their scrambled legs upward.

"Maybe if I could talk to the guy who brought me here. Do you know who he is, maybe his name so I can ask a ward to take me to him?"

She grins. "That would be the most badass of the winter fae. Lysander Nightfrost."

"Lysander Nightfrost." The name rolls well off the tongue. I remember the large shoulders and bulging biceps. "The most badass you say?"

"Damn right. He's the Lord of Winter. Ruler of the Other Side of Hell."

"The what?"

"Hell. You know it's ruled by—"

"Lucifer, yes, a high demon. Not a fae. And Hell is a place of fire, not ice."

"Yes, that's what most people think. Only those who know the ancient lore are aware of the Other Side of Hell. The Kingdom of Ice, or the Winter Realm, which ensures balance."

"Balance?"

"Let's just say that, without it, the world would tip over, and Hell could spread out."

I remember Aunt Miriam losing a word or two on that, but she mostly avoided the subject.

"Think about it, and you'll see it actually makes sense," Edith continues. "The entire universe defines itself by contrast. Light and shadow, water and earth, day and night. How could fire ever exist without ice? How could you ever have one without the other? The universe depends on balance." She bends closer, her breath warming my frozen cheek. "But one thing you *can* tamper with—who rules both sides of Hell, fire and ice. The Fire Realm, the antechamber of Hell, so to say, has been after the rulership of the Winter Realm for many thousands of years. No one knows exactly how many. But Lysander Nightfrost has been strong enough to keep all of that force at bay. That's how powerful he is."

I remember feeling his power radiating from him, and it was unlike anything I'd ever experienced.

"Can he really freeze time along with space?" I sound like a ghost. I'm fading.

"He can freeze time, he can freeze space, and he can freeze the soul inside people—trap it, like in a prison. He's one of the most powerful fae kings out there, even the Grim Reaper is wary of him. Hey, hey, listen." She slaps me again, her palms cracking the layer of frost forming on my skin.

"You start talking now, it's your turn," she urges.

"If you're just trying to keep me awake—"

"Yes, that's exactly what I'm doing. I won't let you fucking die on me."

"If I die here, or if he sends me to the pit, it's the same."

"Your name, lady friend. Now," she demands.

"Arielle," I whisper. "Arielle de Saelaria."

"Arielle de Sealaria." I can hear the awe behind her whisper. "My God. You're a water fae, aren't you?"

"Half-fae," I breathe.

"Jesus Tinkerbell Christ!"

My eyes fall shut, and I succumb to exhaustion. The last thing I hear is Edith's body slamming into the bars as she calls out into the damp hallway. "Somebody! This woman is who Xerxes Blazeborn of the Fire Realm has been looking for all these years, she is The One. And she's DYING."

CHAPTER II

Lysander

I keep looking at the girl lying on red velvet cushions in a crystal bed. Icicles hang from the ceiling like chandeliers all around her, a whole retinue of fae staring down at her sleeping figure. She seems a Snow White in an ice castle setting.

"How come that girl Edith knew who this woman was, and you didn't?" Sandros reproaches. He stands close to the bed with his retinue of guards, big arms crossed over his broad chest, running his armored hand over his chin. "You are the Lord of Winter, brother. How is it possible that you've been around for longer than Lucifer himself can remember, and you didn't know this?"

"The Snowstorm clan, Edith Snowstorm's family, are the lore keepers of all winter fae," I say. "There are many things they know, and we don't. They are the keepers of our history, of our sacred knowledge. Her family must have passed the knowledge down to her."

"Then you should probably free the girl from imprisonment as well, put her to better use. Like tell us more about this pretty thing." He nods his chin at the sleeping Arielle. "You really think she is the one

20

Xerxes has been looking for? She seems so... young and innocent."

I look down at the sleeping girl, and start to cast the spells that send icicles melting, creating water to help her heal from the frost, and regain her strength. I can't open the windows and allow the power of the ocean in, that would be too dangerous. It would give her too much power, and she wouldn't be able to control it.

Along with her strength, the girl also regains her beauty. Jaws drop all around as the present fae watch it happen.

When I first saw Arielle de Saelaria in that fraternity house in the human world she was only a pale shade of what she's turning into now. Her skin, which had taken on the whiteness of death in the dungeon, is turning into the snowy white of a full water fae, blood filling her lips, plumping them up like blooming roses. The ebony of her hair also regains its luster, looking like black rivers spread over her pillow. The white duvet that covers her body slowly begins molding the full curves of the young woman she was before the frost pruned her.

"If she truly is the descendant of the ocean king," Sandros says as he watches the process, "she could basically shape-shift into water, just like others shift into beasts. I suggest you put a containing spell on her, make sure that doesn't happen."

"I blocked out the ocean especially to avoid a surge of power that she wouldn't be able to control. She might hurt herself before she hurts us, though. But I'll put a silver spell on her when she's awake." My magic floats over Arielle's body, connecting her to the icicles, feeding her their energy.

The other aristocrat families draw closer, eager to watch the half fae regain beauty and shine.

"Love spells," Minerva Midwinter says. "She's been doing love spells in the mortal world. It's the best currency for magical creatures there, isn't it? Humans long for nothing more than love. Easy prey for rotten supernaturals."

Humans don't just crave love, they also monger for power, but it's not like Minerva to wait for answers.

"My Lord, if I may," she continues. "We have no proof this woman is who Edith Snowstorm says she is. I suggest we put her to the test, right away."

The others murmur in agreement, not necessarily because they feel the same way, but it's not advisable for the nobles of Winter Court to antagonize Lady Minerva Midwinter. As leader of the oldest and most powerful fae families, she has an uncomfortably heavy presence, to say the least.

But one man resents and despises her enough to challenge her, and that's Sandros.

"How can this girl sustain a test that could kill her, when she's not even conscious? Besides, if she really is the ocean king's descendant, then she isn't a lesser half-breed of fae and human, she also carries the blood of a god. If she gets hurt in the test for lack of care on our part, or basically because of us taking advantage of her weakness, there will be Hell to pay."

Minerva's white-blond hair flashes golden with fury, but she tightens her sharp jaw, her thin lips forming an even thinner line than they normally do.

She'd slap Sandros if he were one of her subjects, but unfortunately for her he's my brother, and my second in command, General over my armies.

"Then I suggest we have a Council meeting in which to decide how to establish her authenticity," she insists. "We won't be able to use her in any way if her origins aren't established beyond the shadow of a doubt."

The girl moans, slowly regaining consciousness. All eyes lock on her pretty face. She can't be any older than twenty, human years. She's gaining glow and beauty by the second. She moves her fingers, her eyebrows quivering before she opens her eyes, revealing beautiful blue irises.

"By the cursed realms," a nobleman mumbles.

The girl is indeed quite a sight with her ebony hair spread over the pillows, and those blue eyes like sapphire, not to mention that she's got the most delicious rose-red mouth. I can sense that many of the men here are salivating to taste her.

My hand clenches over the silver hilt of my dagger. Ice magic starts to radiate from me, and the nobles step back.

"Lysander, what are you doing?" Sandros intervenes, recognizing the danger behind my white knuckles.

"Her magic is bubbling to the surface," I reply under my breath, my eyes fixed on the girl. "She could lose control."

"But—"

"Arielle de Saelaria." I raise my voice, covering Sandros' and all the others' murmurs. "Do you recognize me?"

"Please, don't, just don't put those chains on me again." Her voice is small, faint, and my fist softens on my dagger.

"I won't." I change the tone of my voice, making it sound more accommodating to her. "You're in a castle suite, you're safe, and I won't put you in the dungeon again."

"Are you an angel?" Arielle whispers as she gets up on her elbows, looking fascinated at Minerva, who exudes an aura of magic. She must be quite a vision to a half-fae girl of twenty who's never been in the supernatural world before. All the others fade in the background, allowing her to stare in awe at Minerva in her crimson queen dress, standing tall and proud near the girl's bed.

"An angel? Oh yes, let me show you," Minerva spits through her thin lips, her fingernails sharpening into the icy claws of a winter beast.

"Minerva, step back, now," I command her before she can fully transform into her magic self, which is no pretty sight. Everybody stops breathing, including the girl. Her eyes move to me. She stares at me with an open mouth, keeping a hand over the blanket that covers her and the black wool rags she's still wearing, her hair flowing like a shiny black river framing milky cheeks.

"Pull back your magic, I have this," I tell Minerva.

She hesitates for a few moments, but she doesn't have a choice, she must obey my command. Her glow retracts, along with her claws of ice.

"Arielle." I keep my voice at a calming cadence. Her small hand tightens on the duvet when she hears me, which is why I let go of the dagger and hold out my hand. "I won't hurt you. Nobody here will. But you're no longer in the human world, you're on the Flipside, and here your fae powers are rising quickly. It might become too much, and you might lose your grip on them. You have to stay focused to make sure that doesn't happen."

"Are we—" She looks around as if searching for something. "Are we around water? I can—" She closes her eyes and breathes in deeply. "I can feel it close, I can smell salt in the air. The ocean."

If the windows weren't perfectly sealed to ensure security, she'd hear the crashing waves, too. The ocean has been acting wild and chaotic ever since I brought her, which could be proof that she is indeed the one Xerxes has been looking for. Too bad it's not proof enough.

"We're on the West Coast of the United States, but on the Flipside."

"West Coast, Flipside." Her eyes widen as she understands. "Did we get here through the bottom of the ocean? Aunt Miriam said that's how us water fae can get to the mirror reality. She said that, if we swam to the bottom of the ocean, from there we'd emerge on the surface of the Flipside."

"The ocean is indeed a portal between worlds, as all water is," I reply. "Mirrors can serve as portals as well, but there are only a few of us that can use them, like me and the Prince of Midnight. For the others, there are designated portals, such as the Mariana Trench, the Bermuda Triangle, abandoned cathedrals, and others."

She stares at me as she pieces information together. "You can use mirrors as portals because you're a fae of ice. The mirrored surface of frozen water becomes a portal under your power."

"So the half-breed is regaining her wits quickly," Minerva cuts in. "Wonderful. That means she can take the test."

"By the cursed realms, woman, will you let her at least recover her strength?" Sandros snaps.

Her lips pucker in anger, and her guards tense, ready to pull out their magic and protect her, but so does Sandros and his people.

"Stand down, both of you," I command. Even though Minerva and Sandros keep glaring at each other, their guards heed. "We're not going to withstand many more attacks by the Fire Realm if we fight amongst each other. If we want to stand strong, as we did so far, we must remain united."

Sandros' eyes dart to me, and it's all I need to read his thoughts. Yes, Minerva is abusing her position, and the respect we owe to her family and ancestors, but she's one of us, and a powerful ally.

I turn to the girl lying on the bed. By the cursed realms, she's even more beautiful than a few moments ago. Her fae side grows stronger and brighter on the Flipside.

"Get some rest," I command her, though I keep my tone mild. "Relax. You're safe now, and you'll be well attended to. When you're rested and fed, we'll meet again. There are things we need to talk about."

I turn on my heels and head to the door, my guards preparing to follow, but the half-fae stops me.

"Please, can I ask for something?"

I tilt my head, searching her gaze. "I'm feeling generous."

"The girl from the dungeon." She frowns and swallows, as if it hurts her throat to speak. "Edith. I would like her freed, and joining me, here."

Murmurs of protest echo through the huge room, but I shoot a look at one of the servants. "Do it."

Arielle

THE DOOR OPENS, AND Edith is thrown inside. She lands on all fours, the door slamming back shut before I get to see who brought her.

"Edith, are you all right?" I run over to her, hitching up the folds of my fresh blue dress, and help her up. She has a hard time moving. Seeing her in the light, I realize the poor thing is in even worse shape than I thought back in the dungeon. She's cold and wet as a fish, bruised and frostbitten. "God, you must have been in there a friggin' decade."

"I may well have lost track of time," she mutters, shielding her eyes from the light with her hand.

I help her to the bed, feeling her ribs under her dirty rags. How long has it been since this girl has eaten?

27

"Lysander Nightfrost is a friggin' monster," I spit as I punch the pillows, supporting her as she lies down against them. "You're more dead than alive, how didn't I notice in the dungeon?"

"Because you were worse off than me." She attempts a laugh that degenerates into coughing. "But don't beat yourself up, doll. It felt good to be the stronger one, to feel like I could be of use to someone, so thanks for that. It was good while it lasted."

She grimaces in pain at every move as she tries to find a comfortable position. It's admirable that she tries to keep her humor, but my heart breaks for her.

"God, it's a miracle you didn't die in there," I say as I remove her dirty rags, patch by patch. They're falling apart, they're so worn and frozen, even though now they started to thaw.

"Fae are stronger than humans. Plus, I'm a winter fae, so I can't get pneumonia or other cold caused illnesses, but that bitch Minerva made sure I went through Hell in other ways."

So the woman I thought was an angel is actually as much a monster as Lysander.

I bring a bowl of warm water from the bath chamber, and resume the work of removing Edith's rags, warming the frosted blood from her frostbitten wounds that her clothing sticks to. I grimace, feeling with her as her cheeks twitch, as I unstick the cloth from her skin bit by bit.

"Is it normal for winter fae to get frostbitten?"

"Other powerful winter fae can make that happen. But if you're just asking questions in order to distract me from the pain, you don't have to. Your touch does me good."

"Aunt Miriam taught me a thing or two about healing, but I'm no expert." I smile at her while I dab her wounds with a fresh face towel.

"I'll be right back." I run to the door, holding the folds of my dress up to make sure I don't stumble over the hem. As expected, guards stand to attention as I pull the heavy door open, but there's also a young servant boy ready to attend us. He jumps up from his little stool when he sees me. He's fae by the looks of him, the tips of his spiked ears protruding through his ashen hair. The color marks him as lesser winter fae, or that's what Aunt Miriam told me. Bright gold and silver mark the higher fae, white the middle aristocrats, and ashen the lesser ones.

"I'm gonna need disinfectant and pain killers," I tell him in a friendly tone. Every underdog is my friend in here. "Do you think you can help me with that?"

He stares at me confused. "I'm sorry Milady. We don't use those things here."

Edith laughs, drawing my attention. "This is the supernatural world, Arielle de Saelaria," her voice echoes over from the bed. "You heal people with the power of your magic, or with spells. Your nature, your hands, and your words, those are the only medicine you'll get in the supernatural realms."

"But what about magic plants? Aunt Miriam said witches—"

"Witches are inferior to fae, they need 'tools' like herbs, bones and voodoo puppets. We're higher supernaturals."

"If I may suggest," the young servant says, drawing closer to the door as if avoiding that the guards hear. "Feel the magic in your body, Milady," he whispers. "If you are who Milord thinks you are, you have a wealth of it to tap into."

I can feel magic rippling deep in my core, more than I felt in the mortal world, like it's more tangible, but it's still not close to what the fae lore says fae kind can do.

"I feel *some* magic inside me, but I can't seem to bring it out." I squeeze my eyes shut, as if cutting back on my sense of sight would strengthen my other senses, especially the sixth one I need in order to tap into my magic.

"Don't try to grab it," a powerful male voice says. My eyes snap open. It's the Lord of Winter, standing right in front of me, the servant boy making himself small beside him. The guards' heavy armor clamors as they kick their heels, the metallic sound echoing against the hallway. He must have formed here out of thin air, otherwise the guards would have reacted sooner, right?

"Just feel it, let it bubble up to the surface," he says in a deep calm voice like the dark depths of the ocean.

I want to scream at him and beat his chest for what he put Edith through, but I'm not sure that's such a good idea.

"Negative feelings poison your magic." The more he approaches me, I instinctively walk backwards.

He's like a block of muscles, with vambraces of silver wrapped on his big forearms. His torso is naked, but a sort of mail is wrapped around his waist, fading upwards into his skin like the scales of an ice dragon. It changes color from light blue to silver as he walks, and it appears to be crawling slowly up his body. Wait, don't tell me his flesh is turning into armor. He's beautiful and terrible, like an angel of war.

"I can feel both your hate and your awe, Arielle," he says, now so close I can feel the cold coming off his skin. "Neither is good for your powers."

"And what am I supposed to feel," I say through my teeth, "when I have a cruel bastard like you in front of me?"

He breathes in, his large chest rising to the level of my forehead. Everything about him radiates power, being a king is in his blood—if that is what flows through his frozen veins.

"This isn't about me," he says. "It's about helping Edith."

"Edith wouldn't be in this wretched situation, if it weren't for your sadistic treatment of her." Unable to control myself, I hit him in the chest with the sides of my fists. They crash into a body that is as hard as an iceberg. I can hear the young servant gasp in the background, terrified that I dared charge on the great king of the Winter Realm.

But the king simply grabs my hands in his own, so large that they swallow my fists completely. His silver vambraces glisten in the cold morning sunlight.

"I suggest you stop that, it's not going to help anybody."

"How could you keep her there in her state?" My eyes blaze into his. He stares down at me without blinking, but there's something more than fury in his icy blue eyes. Something like curiosity, and maybe even surprise.

"You can ask all the questions you like, just not yet. If the girl's state is so important to you, why not start to work on it right away."

My blood boils despite the cold he emanates.

"How can I feel anything but rage when I look at you?"

"You're a complex, sophisticated being, Arielle. Your feelings are never simple, they're a cocktail of emotions. Reach for something that feels pleasant, or, if that's not possible, just less provoking than rage and hatred."

My eyes are hot with the need to punish him as they glide over the chiseled features of his face, his sharp cheekbones, his square jaw. He's a vision of cold masculinity. I feel all sorts of things as I look at him, and I feel like I have to make a choice—hate him, or drool over him.

"The only thing I feel when I look at you, Great King, is the need to punish you for what you did to both Edith and me."

"Does that need feel good to you, or does it give you a bad vibe?" he says in a calm, composed tone.

"It feels good."

"All right then, tap into it."

I furrow my brow. "You mean you're okay with that? With knowing that I hate your guts?"

"You cannot control your own feelings, how could I or anyone else ever control them?" Instead of offense, I hear ancient wisdom in his voice. He frees my fists from his big hands, and places them on my shoulders. His touch is surprisingly warm, even though he radiates cold.

"Now harness your power."

"It's hard to do while I have you in front of me."

"Then feel free to face away."

He doesn't have to tell me twice. I turn to look at Edith, who's now sitting on the queenly bed under the canopy, her patchy rags not covering her as much as they should. But it seems she's too taken with Lysander Nightfrost to care about that. She stares at him like she's just seen a god.

"Edith." I snap my fingers in front of her eyes.

"I'm sorry. It's just that I've never seen the King in the light before, not in this form."

"In this form? What do you mean?"

"In his body, as fae. I only ever saw him in his full magic shape."

"It'll help if your senses make contact with the ocean," Nightfrost interrupts her, opening the big high windows. The glass must be especially strong, multi-layered, because the wild sound of the ocean hits me like an avalanche as soon as that barrier is out of the way.

I close my eyes, my body tensing, trying to contain the surge of power inside me. It flares in my core, and great joy fills me. I open my arms, letting the magic mount along with my joy until it fills me to the brim. It feels fantastic until it becomes too much, and I start to lose control.

"God, I won't be able to contain it."

"Channel it through your limbs to your fingertips," Lysander says behind me, his tone calming, like a balm. "Keep your hands down, let the excess magic flow to the ground first, you need to dose it well before you use it on your patient."

Aunt Miriam told me that all fae are natural healers, through their magic, but I was never able to harness so much of it in the mortal world, not even enough to heal my own wounds; well, maybe that, but only occasionally. Aunt Miriam was the one who took care of me when I got sick, and I even saw a doctor once. But she did everything to avoid that because of the differences in anatomy and chemistry between half-fae and full humans.

Now the magic flowing through my limbs demands all of my attention. When it starts to crackle in my palms I jump, but Lysander comes behind me, giving out energy that balances me. Silver strings start flowing from my fingertips.

"Now," he says gently. "Place your finger over a wound, and direct your healing magic to it. You'll know which the healing magic is."

Strangely, I can easily pick from the cocktail of powers that twist and turn inside my core. They're wild, untamable, and I know I wouldn't be able to contain them if it weren't for the huge fae king behind me keeping things under control.

"Go ahead," Edith whispers, her eyes still moving between Lysander and me. I can sense the young servant by the door staring as well, standing still, but with a deeply interested stare.

It's not long until all of Edith's wounds are closed, and she lies on her back, falling asleep under Lysander's guidance. He turns to address the servant.

"Bring food, essences and oils for fragrance therapy. It will help young Lady Snowstorm regain her strength."

"How come I don't even feel tired," I whisper as I stare at my hands. I can balance my power better by the minute. "How is this possible?" I spin on my heels to face Lysander, and I find him measuring me from head to toes. I become instantly self-aware, feeling naked in my pale blue dress. The corset pushes up my breasts, causing them to form quite a sizeable swell, and it squeezes my waist to create a contrast. If I felt like a princess the first time I put it on and spun around in the mirror, I feel like a deer in the headlights now.

"Your powers are growing quickly," he says. "I'm going to have to contain your magic now, or it will overwhelm you."

"Contain it? No, not now that I just discovered it. I have to learn how to use it, please."

"Don't worry, you will still have command of it, but you won't have to deal with so much at once."

"You mean you'll limit my power."

"You're new at this. Things could get out of control."

I cross my arms, not entirely unaware of the way my breasts are squeezed forth, pushing up. A sapphire necklace covers my chest down to the line between my breasts, but his ice-blue eyes still fall on them. It sends a ripple of pleasure right down between my legs— don't tell me I like being admired by this beautiful monster. I stare harder into his eyes to get a better grip on myself.

"You got me out of the dungeon, but I'm still a prisoner, aren't I?"

"Of course you are." He glances over my head at the quietly sleeping Edith. "But it's up to you to keep this prison cozy and luxurious for both you and your new friend, so I advise that you refrain from antagonizing me."

I press my lips together. I guess I can't afford to piss him off.

"Why did take me out of the dungeon?"

"I'll let young Lady Snowstorm explain that to you. I think you'll take it better from her than from me. Besides." He gives me a once over, one that feels intended to be cold and forbidding, and yet it's filled with a curiosity that seems new to the great King. "This is probably the last time we speak to each other in person. I'm the king of the Winter Realm, and you are to address me as Milord from now on, as all my subjects do."

No shit. I scoff and jut out my chin. "As far as I remember I'm a water fae—half-fae—so you are *not* *my* king."

"Arielle." He holds out his hands for mine, his energy tugging at me in a way I can't resist. I unlock my arms and place my hands in his. They're really small in comparison, which makes me feel things I shouldn't. I never realized I was into super big guys, or is it his powers, playing tricks on me? "You went against supernatural law, and it cannot be blamed on lack of knowledge. Your Aunt Miriam taught you well—and you would surely like me to keep believing that, otherwise she'll end up in my dungeon, too, for having neglected to teach a half-fae the rules."

"She taught me everything," I react quickly. "I made every decision knowing full well what I was doing."

"You used magic like love spells to fulfill humans' wishes in exchange for material gain. That puts you in my power for punishment. So you see, it's in your best interest to acknowledge me as *your* king, and do your best to get in my good graces."

You gotta be shitting me. The bastard is cocky as fuck.

"Don't you judge me. I did what I had to do to survive. I have student loans, and Aunt Miriam is working herself to death, in her human form, to pay them off."

"You could have done the same to help her with those debts. Work, like a human. Get a student job. Instead you chose the easy way."

Anger stains my skin, making me burn everywhere. "You think you understand it all, don't you, entitled bastard." At the door, the terrified young servant gasps. He returned with the oils and fragrances. "A normal job wouldn't have brought in half the money. Aunt Miriam wanted me to focus on my studies, so I did what I thought was best to help her with the burden—really help her, not just scrap a few pennies together. But you would throw children in the dungeon for breaking a plate." I look back at Edith. "Look at her, only a teenager for a fae. Whatever she's done, it can't be so bad that she deserves being imprisoned and made to suffer like that. You're a monster."

"I didn't put Edith Snowstorm in the dungeon," Lysander says quietly. He looks over me at the sleeping Edith. "I didn't even know she was in there until the Wards came to me with the information she'd given them on you. But I will find out who imprisoned her, and why."

I open my mouth to say something, but he focuses his cold blue eyes on me, his irises filling with the glow of bright ice. A new magic wraps around me, this time not made of frosty vines and thorns, but small silver tattoos like the writing on runes. They emerge from my skin and start snaking over my body.

"What the hell," I shriek, jumping away from him, panicking as I look down at myself.

"The chains for your magic," he explains. "They won't be half as unpleasant as the last ones, in fact, they may feel good on your skin, because they also protect you from the magic of other fae. Not many here are your friends. But you'll only be able to use your own magic at a minimum."

"Why must you limit me like this?"

"I can't let you run around with that kind of power. I couldn't do it even if I trusted you. You're a water fae with the ocean just outside your window, basically a toddler with a loaded gun."

I do my best to hold his glowing gaze. "Milord, a lot has happened in such a short time, I must say I'm confused as fuck."

The servant drops the oils he was pretending to arrange on the bedside table, while Lysander cocks an eyebrow, raising his strong chin.

"Excuse my language, but it's the way it is. One thing I need to know, and that I need to know now is why you took me out of the dungeon, and started to treat me like a friggin' princess?"

"The time will come for answers."

"Well, forgive me, if I can't just quietly wait for such a time. I'm worried about what's coming at me."

He hesitates, the large chamber filling with silence and the sound of the ocean.

"One thing I can promise you, Arielle," Lysander says, the silver symbols caressing my skin while he speaks. "You will be protected. I will keep you completely safe for as long as you're in my power."

"Oh. You won't be keeping me indefinitely?"

Instead of answering he turns around, and heads for the exit, his shiny blond hair falling in beautiful waves to his broad, muscular shoulders. My gaze keeps glued to his back, his muscles snaking under his white-bluish skin. He's the most beautiful creature I've ever seen, so I suppose it's normal to stare. It's not like I should be ashamed of myself, should I? Not even for staring at his muscular ass as the mail pants hug it. Strength, ice and metal, the combination stirs me.

I watch King Lysander Nightfrost leave. He leaves a trail of winter scent behind, and a strange emptiness in my lower belly.

The young servant stares at me with big eyes for moments after Lysander exits the chamber. The boy is unassuming for a fae, but he'd definitely be a beauty among humans, even if he looks a bit of a nerd.

"What's your name?" I inquire in a quiet voice. He glances over his shoulder at the guards outside.

"Come on, it's an innocent question." I smile, leaning my head against the marble bedpost.

"Pablo, Milady."

I frown. "That's a human name."

"I was born in the mortal realm, like you."

"Oh." My eyebrows rise as I make the connection. "That means you're the result of broken rules, too."

"Your wit is quick, Milady."

"Did the King punish you, too when you were found?"

He shakes his head. "He's strict, but not absurd. It wasn't my fault. It was my parents'." He looks anxiously behind him. "I'm sorry, Milady, but I'm needed."

"Wait."

But he doesn't. He shuts the door behind him a little too hard. I do need to know why Lysander freed me from the dungeon, because I'm dead certain he has a secret agenda.

I sit on the bed next to Edith, caressing her forehead and her long hair that's slowly turning from white to silver as she regains her healthy glow. So she is higher fae after all. She looks peaceful, sleeping deeply, like she probably hasn't slept in a very long time, tormented by the cold and pain in that dungeon. My stomach churns at the thought that someone had the heart to put her in that place.

Aunt Miriam comes to mind, too, and worry rises in my throat. Did I manage to convince Lysander that she's not to blame for anything I've done? I swear to God that if he hurts her, I'll make him pay, if it's the last thing I do.

Edith stirs, and I draw closer to her.

"You're fine, sweetheart, you're all right."

She opens her soft brown eyes, murmuring something. When it finally makes sense, my blood starts   to   boil.

CHAPTER III

Lysander

"

Do it?" Minerva repeats what I told the guard, frustration staining her cheeks. "You basically told that man and the servant she is now their mistress, and they have to indulge her whims!"

"If she really is who Edith claims she is, I want her satisfied and willing to cooperate," I reply calmly.

"Cooperate with what," Minerva exclaims, spreading out her arms to make sure everybody looks at her. She fixes me with intense silver eyes as she speaks, as if provoking me, her golden hair shining like a halo. "You think any amount of luxury and comforts will have her agreeing to being traded over to Xerxes Blazeborn, Lord of Fire? He fucking rules the realm just before Hell, the antechamber of the pit. No person in their right mind would agree to that, no matter what you give them."

"First of all," Sandros' voice booms into the hall as he joins the gathering, the grand doors closing behind him as he and his retinue of guards advance into the hall. Their metal boots and natural body armor clamor as they march over. The clusters of aristocrats forming the Winter Council move to the sides, making room.

"My brother needs to ensure the girl is in perfect shape for Xerxes. He might be furious she was treated like a prisoner, and left to freeze to death in a dungeon. He could use that as a pretext to continue the war, *after* he got his hands on her."

"If the tales about what he wants with her are true," Minerva says as she gracefully takes her place at the Council table, "then he could care less if we delivered her to him half dead."

"My brother is right, Minerva," I say. "No matter what Xerxes' true desires or intentions are, he could use that as a pretext to continue the war anyway."

"Well, that is the reason why we gathered here today, isn't it, to decide what to do with her, how to make best use of her," Sandros says, stepping onto the dais and walking to his place by my side. He keeps a hand on the hilt of his magic silver blade, the gauntlet shining in the icicle light.

The aristocrats curl their noses at him. Sandros is dark and intimidating, and his looks are definitely not those of a winter fae. The dark color of his hair along with his intense golden eyes give him a slight demonic appearance, and that's why the Aristocrat Council of the Winter Realm originally banished him; he's only half winter fae, and it seems his mother was from the Fire Realm. He's a half-breed that stands for the breaking of an old, sacred rule. If there is anything more frowned upon than fae mixing with humans, it's fae mixing with 'inconceivably incompatible' fae, like fire and ice. It would have been okay if my father's second wife would have been a water fae, that's compatible, but Sandros is the result of a clandestine

43

affair that has never really been proven. I recognized him officially as my brother after our father's death, especially because it was our father's last wish. Every time Sandros joins the Council I think of that day.

They all wait for me sit. The outer layer of my skin turns into the iced mailed armor that marks my status, leaving only my neck and my head free. I take my seat on the grand ice throne, my hands that are now ice gauntlets resting on the broad sides.

Once I take this seat, little is left of Lysander. I am now fully the king, the Lord of Winter, and every decision I make must be in the best interest of my people, not mine or my next of kin's. All emotion shuts down.

"Maybe we should bring the girl, too," Sandros murmurs under his breath.

"I don't see why," the aristocrat next to him says. "It's not like she has a say in this."

"It's her future that's being decided," Sandros growls.

"She is a prisoner, even if she's being treated like nobility," Minerva argues. "She broke the law, serving humans' lust in exchange for money."

"That's not what she was doing," another fae says, even though quietly, as not to anger Minerva. It's not easy for people to sustain a point of view different from hers in these meetings. That's how Sandros ended up on her black list, not that he was ever on the white one due to his supposed origins.

"She explained why she used her magic in the mortal world," I say. All eyes dart to me, because it's unusual for the Lord of Winter to do anything but listen and judge in these situations, and then speak the verdict. But I'm the only person the girl talked to about what she did and why. "Her gigs helped pay off her student loans, and unburden her aunt."

"Oh, how moving," Minerva reacts. "So she can justify her actions. I haven't heard a more wishy washy explanation in hundreds of years, I can't believe she actually thought it would work." She puffs and waves her hand.

"Yes, about that," I say. "I'd be curious as to the reason why Edith Snowstorm was left to freeze in the dungeon. I ordered that she be arrested and taken to her family, where she would spend the next decade as punishment for having crossed over. She never performed any magic in the mortal realm, so I decided she would not be imprisoned here. Only the members of this Council are authorized to throw fae into the dungeon, the Wards wouldn't have obeyed anyone else. I demand to know who of you it was."

People look at each other clueless. In the end, all heads turn to Minerva. Her thin red lips pucker.

"It was me," she admits, even though I know she wouldn't have done it if it wasn't for the peer pressure. "But this Council didn't come together today to discuss Ms. Snowstorm, but Arielle de Saelaria."

"We discuss whatever I consider needs to be discussed." I raise my voice over the hall. "While by ancient law using magic in the mortal world is strictly forbidden, no matter the circumstances, the law for simply crossing over and not making a show of magic powers is much milder. Does Edith Snowstorm stand accused of anything I'm not aware of?"

Minerva speaks up, and she does it with an air of entitlement.

"She crossed over to the human world, and drew attention through her fae beauty, *intentionally*," she says. "She wasn't getting enough attention among fae men, so she sought it among the mortals, who are less used to such striking looks."

"Hardly enough of a reason to subject her to freezing, starvation and other kinds of suffering in the dungeon."

"I was just taking the ancient law seriously, Milord," Minerva says.

"Returning to the matter at hand," Sandros chimes in. "Doing the same with Arielle de Saelaria would be too dangerous. I suggest we keep her in luxury, make sure Xerxes doesn't use her mistreatment as a pretext." He pauses and takes in a deep breath. I know him well enough to understand he's about to say something that will set the others on fire. "I must also argue in favor of bringing her here, to attend this meeting. We can make all the plans we want, if she's not in on them, she's not going to play along."

"She might not play along anyway," another voice rises from the Council. "We're talking about giving her over to Xerxes, for fuck's sakes."

"I'm not sure that giving her over is the right thing to do," I say. All Council members stare at me with large eyes.

"I thought that much was set in stone," Minerva hisses through her teeth.

"I never thought I'd ever say this," Sandros grunts. "But I agree with Minerva. If what we want is to end the war with Xerxes, we have to do this. We have something that's super valuable to him, and we put it to the best use possible."

"Yes, but trading her over without knowing exactly what he intends to do with her powers is extremely risky. We need a special oath from him, something that will compel him to fulfill it," I say.

"What are you talking about, brother, all fae are bound to their oaths. We're all compelled to fulfill them."

"I may remind you, brother, that Xerxes is the next in line to Lucifer's throne in Hell. He is a master of trickery, just like Lucifer."

Murmur ripples through the gathering.

"There are oaths that cannot be cheated, like blood oaths," the oldest Council member says in a cracked voice. He's ancient, experienced, and highly cunning. "A blood oath can bind even archangels, let alone high fae. The problem with this kind of oaths is that it implies exchanging blood—Xerxes would cut his wrist and give you a few drops to keep, and you would have to give your blood to him. I suppose I don't have to tell you what that means."

It means that Xerxes would then be able to perform some nasty magic on me, even create something like a voodoo doll and manipulate me from a distance, but then again, so could I with his blood. I shake my head.

"He'll never agree to it. And who could blame him?"

"But it's the only way to make sure he fulfills his promises, and never tries to overcome the Winter Realm," Minerva says enthusiastically. "Just imagine,

Lysander. You have the one thing Xerxes wants. Arielle de Saelaria, descendant of the ocean king. He's been searching for her for so long that he'll give you anything in exchange. You'll have one hell of an advantage in your negotiations with him. You can even use her to rip a blood oath from him, and that's— Come on, Lysander, you have to see it, it's huge. You could get the world from him."

I stare blankly ahead of me as I turn this in my head.

"All right. I'll take the risk. My blood will be in his hands, but his in mine, too. Still, it will be better if the girl is in on it. We'll need her to cooperate, which means we have to motivate her."

"You mean more like blackmail her," Sandros says.

"I agree," Minerva puts in. "But all of this is only going to work if she really is who Edith Snowstorm says she is. We have to put her to the test."

A strange feeling tugs at my heart. "It's too dangerous."

"Not to mention it's barbaric," Sandros ads, not even trying to suppress his anger. "Remember all the deaths that kind of test brought about back in the days of Salem in the mortal realm."

Minerva holds her ground. "Yes, but this isn't the mortal realm, and Arielle de Saelaria is not a witch. She's supposedly the very daughter of the ocean." She turns to the Council, speaking forcefully, determined to persuade them. "Imagine we go through all the trouble of arranging a meeting with Xerxes, getting him to agree to a blood oath, and it turns out the girl is nothing but a half-breed with mere mermaid powers, able only to lure weak men into the beds of her girlfriends. He'll be so furious, it will make the war even bloodier."

My jaw clenches. I never shied away from war, and I would never shy away from a confrontation with Xerxes. But I can't put my people in danger, I can't allow the shadow of destruction, death and decay to fall over the Winter Realm. Xerxes could even attack the Flipside, and that would be a catastrophe for humans, since the Flipside is only a step away from their world.

More members of the Council vote that the girl be brought in, and subjected to the test. But why in the cursed realms do I feel this nagging tug in my chest when the decision falls? It shouldn't bother me—subject her to the test, send word to Xerxes if she's the one; if she dies in the process, it's the way it is. The cause is greater than any one of us, the stakes are higher than ever.

Sandros stands up, his men standing to attention behind him.

"It's settled then," he says. "I'll fetch the girl."

Arielle

"A TEST?" I RAISE MY eyebrows at the dark, wild-looking fae in front of me. "May I ask what it consists of? And shouldn't I have some time to prepare?"

He looks me up and down, his armor glinting on his body. Just like in Lysander's case, I realize it's his flesh that turns into icy metal. But unlike the king, he makes an apologetic grimace when his guards come forth and grab me.

"Hey." I struggle, but they're too strong. "You can't just throw me straight into it."

"Where are you taking her?" Edith says behind me. She gets off the bed, still moving with some difficulty. "I'm coming along."

"No, you're not," the dark haired fae says. "We can't afford anything distracting Miss de Saelaria. She's going to need all her strength, and all of her focus."

"What the hell are going to do with me?" I shriek as the guards push me towards the door.

"You're putting her through Love of the Ocean, aren't you?" Edith calls out behind me. I can hear the panic in her voice.

"We have to make sure she is who you say she is," the fae replies.

"You don't need to make sure of anything. You have my word. My family are the keepers of ancient lore, I know what I'm talking about. Actually, I assume full responsibility. If it turns out she isn't the ocean king's descendant, I'm willing to pay with my head."

"I'm sorry to be so blunt, but your head is of little value, Lady Snowstorm," the rugged fae cuts her off. "And taking the test is a must, the stakes are too high."

"What stakes? What the fuck are you talking about?" I cry. The guards have stopped with me by the door, waiting for the fae to give further instruction, but he can't seem to walk away from this intense exchange with Edith.

"You know the ancient lore," he says. "You know who's after the descendant of the ocean king, and why."

"You can't be fucking serious," Edith manages, looking daggers at the fae. "You can't be thinking of handing her over."

"Anybody care to explain to me what's happening?"

But the fae turns his back on Edith, and leads the way out of the room. I struggle to free myself, but the guards' mailed hands dig into my arms as they drag me forward. I see over my shoulder how Edith starts after us with a wild look in her soft brown eyes, but Pablo the servant scurries over and holds her back.

I get to see the look of worry on the ashen-haired boy's face. At least he's going to make sure she doesn't get hurt trying to help me out of a clearly helpless situation. I direct my attention to the warrior fae leading the way.

"Please, where are you taking me, what's going to happen?"

He doesn't answer. They drag me along hallways, through cloisters that seem sculpted out of marble, ice and crystal, sparkling as if studded with diamonds. Beauty without meaning to me. All I can think about is that I'm about to die.

The salty scent of the ocean hits my senses, causing power to surge in my core, but the silver drawings on my skin react. The power dampens, remaining only a dull thud in my lower belly. The fae pushes open a set of grand doors, and we enter a room so large it seems a cathedral. I realize it's a council room, judging by the table up on the crystal dais. Archways open behind it, allowing in the scent and sound of the ocean.

Lysander presides over the Council like a king of ice and metal. The sight of him is enough to knock the air from my lungs. His long blond hair seems a river of gold flowing to his shoulders, and his sharp features give the perfect finish to his air of authority.

The guards throw me on the dais stairs, my knees knocking into a sharp edge. I grunt and curse at the impact, as I'm sure the edge sliced the skin on my knee. Someone claps their hands.

"The supposed daughter of the ocean." I raise my eyes to identify Minerva Midwinter, who seems a malefic fairy in crimson. "Finally, the moment of truth. Now we'll know if you really are as valuable as Edith Snowstorm claims. If you really are the one who can finally end the war between fire and ice."

"What the hell are you talking about, you fucking lunatic," I spit, spurred on by the sharp pain in my knee, and by the anger and frustration at being treated like a lesser creature by these entitled bastards.

She measures me up and down with unmasked contempt. Her thin lips form a distorted line that looks almost ugly, even though she's fae and therefore inherently beautiful.

I manage to stand, hands gripping tightly to the folds of my blue dress. "What are you going to do to me?"

Many rigid eyes watch me from the Council. I lock my gaze on Lysander, driven by a strange feeling that I can rely on him for support, but it turns out that's just plain stupid of me. He's the one who signals the two guards to grab me by my arms, and hoist me onto the ledge of an archway that opens to the ocean. It all happens fast, and they let me go abruptly, which causes me to flail my arms in order to keep balance.

I look down at the raging waves, grabbing onto a side column to keep steady. The ledge is only wide enough for my feet. If I move an inch, I'll fall into the waves that rise to swallow me with their foamy crests. Thousands of tiny droplets mist my face, and it feels surprisingly good in all this madness.

"It would seem the ocean feels her presence," Minerva comments. "The waves rise for her like hungry beasts." She's at a distance of two archways from me, leaning over to look down. Then her eyes find me with evil anticipation.

"You're not going to throw me in there, are you?"

"What would be the problem?" Minerva says with a grin. "If you're truly the daughter of the ocean, the water is only going to bring you back up, rising you on a throne of water and foam."

"You're insane."

"It's the ancient lore."

"The ancient lore often speaks in riddles and fables. You can't take it literally."

My eyes dart around, desperate for someone to react and save me. They stop on Lysander. He has to step in for me, he just has to. But the ice king doesn't move from his throne of icicles that resemble blades.

"Milord," I plead, my voice shaking. With one hand I still hold on to the column, while I reach out to him with the other, begging for him to help me. "You can't let them do this, it'll kill me. It's true that I am a water fae, but you put this spell on me, with the drawings." I stretch out my arm for the Council to see. "My magic is chained, I cannot use it."

"That's exactly the point," Lysander says in a deep kingly voice that fills the hall. "You won't be able to use your magic properly, otherwise you'd help yourself out of the water, or even disappear in it, swim all the way to another continent if you wanted to. I know you've never experienced this in the mortal world, but you're a water fae, developing full powers here, on the Flipside. We need to strip you of your powers in order to determine if you really are the daughter of the ocean. The ocean has to be the only one acting now, showing us the truth."

"Jesus Christ," I cry. "You're ancient, magical creatures, you're supposed to be wise. Instead you're medieval blood-thirsty inquisitors on a witch hunt."

The wind blows through the folds of my dress, the salty ocean air enveloping me.

"It's time," Minerva says. The guards approach, slowly, as if to prolong the torture.

"If I'm about to die, I might as well tell you this, Lady Minerva." Spite curls my lips. "You're the ugliest fae I've ever seen."

Rage lights up her face. She marches over so quickly I barely see her move, and pushes me off the archway. I flail and scream as I fall, the wind blowing sharply against my back. Black strands of hair whip over my face.

I know that when my back hits the ocean surface it's going to feel like hitting concrete. It's going to break my spine and, if by some miracle I don't die, I'm gonna break so many bones I'll wish I'd never been born. And all because of King Lysander Nightfrost. He did this to me.

I race toward the water, my arms outstretched to the grey sky heavy with thunderclouds, the wind sharp against the back of my thighs, my hair whipping my face. The sound of my gown flapping deafens me. The silver markings glow brighter the closer I come to the water, snaking on my body, keeping my power locked in my core so that I can't use it.

The moment comes. I brace myself for the impact, pressing my eyes shut, but the sensation I expect doesn't come. The foam embraces me like cushions. But the water wraps around me like tentacles, pulling me in. I landed softly, but now the force of the ocean sucks me under, the salty water filling my nostrils, and my mouth. It replaces the air in my lungs. I panic and fight it, but then something awakens deep inside me, and I still.

I stop fighting, giving in to the ocean's embrace. I let it fill my lungs, which, surprisingly, is only unpleasant for a second. Then I feel myself become one with the water, as if my very flesh becomes fluid. Only then do I feel the water pushing me up, forming a sort of cocoon around my body.

I emerge out into the air. I take in a deep breath out of instinct, which burns my lungs. I cough and double over, but the water grips me tightly, and pushes me upward. I'm soaking wet, my hair clinging to my face and shoulders, my dress heavy on my body. The higher this cocoon of water rises, the colder I feel, and by the time I reach the archway from which I fell, my teeth are chattering.

I search for Lysander's face among the Council members, who are now gathered by the archway. Lysander looks desolate, but when he sees me his eyes regain their glint, and his entire body straightens from his slumped position. I grin. Yes, you bastard, I'm back. And you'll pay for what you put me through.

Minerva Midwinter stands with her back at the archway, but she turns around now, probably because of Lysander's reaction. And when she sees me here, appearing to sit on a throne of waves and foam, her jaw drops.

"I'll be damned," she whispers.

My shaking turns violent as my body regains its original density, returning to its composition of flesh and bone. They watch the process with open mouths and wide eyes, while I experience all sorts of new sensations on the inside of my body. I know for a fact that I'll never be the same person again, not after what happened tonight. I experienced too many transformations, and now I grasp how much that can change a person.

The water sets me back on the archway. I grab onto the column for safety, but this time a whole bunch of fae, Council members, rush over to help me down. I can feel the ocean water still whirling behind me, but the moment I set foot on the cold marble floor, it descends. I hear it splash against the rocks at the base of this castle. It's a miracle I didn't crash into them when I fell.

"She is the one," one of the fae members exclaims, enthusiasm and hope in his voice. Everyone is trying to touch me, with a few exceptions. Minerva and the representatives of her clan.

She stands aside with arms crossed, the crimson sleeves of her dress hanging from her forearms. If looks could kill, hers would surely finish me now. As for Lysander, he stands in front of his throne, wrapped in his majestic mailed armor that wraps his warrior muscles, and that appears to be made of a combination of silver and ice. We hold each other's gaze, him standing there like the king he is, me bracing myself, trembling violently from the cold, a bunch of worshipping hands all over me. Finally, Lysander smiles.

"Arielle de Saelaria," he decrees, "you truly are the daughter of the ocean, the ocean king's only living descendant."

"F-f—f-fuck you," I stutter.

Some councilmen gasp and murmur, but Lysander just starts down the stairs as if he didn't hear me. "You will be treated as a queen at my Court. I am sorry you had to go through this test in order to establish your true identity, but now there is no doubt in the world left, and you will be given your rightful place among the fae noblemen."

I can feel Minerva's glare. She would crack my skull open if she could. Is it weird, that I feel satisfaction at having my status elevated before her eyes?

Now Lysander stands in front of me, his impressive blue eyes locked on my face.

"One thing I can promise you now, Arielle," he says. There's solemnity in his voice. "You'll be honored as a high fae from now on, and no one will ever look down on you again as a half-breed."

"No sh-sh-shit."

Some of the Council members gasp at my nerve, but most of them are still busy worshipping me. I slowly start to become aware of what happened—I just proved to everybody, myself included, that I am the descendant of the ocean god, of the entity the world knows as Poseidon, even though the truth of him is somewhat different.

Which also means I'm not only human and fae, but I also carry the blood of a god. I start to remember a few things Aunt Miriam said about the Trinity of Blood, hybrids that carry the genetic makeup of three kinds of creatures, not only two. But that's where my brain stops thinking. I'm insanely cold, and my body is still going through changes.

Lysander winds an arm around me, scooping me away from the worshipping hands. Every inch of me wants me to slap his arm away, kick and punch him for what he put me through, make him suffer.

But there's no fighting Lysander, at least not in my state. I actually find myself welcoming the support as he leads me back to the room I occupied before, followed by a retinue of guards. I'm relieved to see Edith, chewing her fingernails nervously on the bed. She seems to snap back to life when she sets her eyes on me.

"Arielle, thank God," she shrieks and rushes over. She throws her arms around me, holding me tightly for moments. Her warm body sends heat into my frozen flesh like needles. Compared to me, she feels hot as a stove. I cringe, and she disengages, helping me to the bed. I walk hunch-backed, bracing myself.

"Why did the king come here with you?" she whispers in my ear, looking behind as Lysander follows us like a shadow.

"I d-d-d-didn't f-f-f-fuckin' invite him."

"Wait." She grabs my shoulders, her fingers drilling painfully into my frozen flesh.

"If you're here it means... By the blessed realms! The ocean rose you back to the castle tower on a throne of water!"

My lips tremble in an attempt to smile. Edith pulls me in a tight hug, then helps me out of the dress— tearing bits of it in the process. She's quick to grab the duvet to tuck me in, and cover my nakedness.

"I'll take it from here," Lysander's powerful voice vibrates inside my skull. As he moves closer Edith stands from the bed, staring at him as he takes her place by my side.

I'm lying down on the soft warm pillows, looking up at Lysander. I would cringe and hiss like a cat that doesn't want to be touched, but the bed feels good, and I can't bring myself to protest when Lysander raises a hand over my face.

Right before my eyes, his silver-ice gauntlet transforms into the hand of the warrior. He touches a finger to my forehead, and in the moment of contact I become sharply aware of my body. I shudder violently, clutching the duvet to my chest, my hands balled into frozen fists. I become aware of my nakedness.

"Relax," Lysander whispers, his breath touching my face.

I close my eyes and breathe in his scent of frost, and freshness, and magic winters. He now touches me with his entire hand, cupping my cheek. I feel small and fragile against his big rough palm, but what surprises me most right now is how warm he feels.

"I'm going to restore your body temperature," he says in a voice that calms me down, making me feel accepting of everything. "I would have already started on our here here but you needed to lie down, and be comfortable."

"Bring her some food, please," he tells Edith, big hand still on my face, and his eyes fixed on mine. "Hearty food, croissants, maybe a latte—you like latte, yes, Arielle."

I nod faintly. Anything that will warm me on the inside, and latte sounds fantastic.

"Pablo will help you, he'll show you to the royal kitchen. He'll know what to choose."

Edith hurries to the door to meet the boy, leaving me alone with the ice king. He now puts both hands on my face, moving his eyes down to my lips, then to my neck. The lower he goes, the faster I breathe, my body growing hotter. I can feel the blood flush into my chest. His gaze feels like a caress.

His blond hair falls over the chiseled sides of his face as he looks down at me, and I think I read something in his eyes, that I see intrigue in his eyes. Like he's curious about my body.

But I'm sure the ice king has experienced lust before. A king like him, beautiful and terrible, with the body of an ice god, women must throw themselves at him. I saw the covert lusty stares that Minerva witch gave him, too, and now I wonder if they actually have something going with each other.

But why do I care? Why do I feel like this while his eyes caress their way down my body? I breathe fast, my blood running all through me as I feel those big warrior hands on my skin. They are the hands skilled at bringing death, hands that I should fear and shriek away from. Instead, here I am, losing myself to his touch, heating up as his hands slide all over my body like he owns me.

I arch my back, pushing my head into the pillow and losing a moan. My body is uncomfortably hot, making me squirm with my legs.

"Please, that's enough," I tell him, and he removes his hands from my body. My temperature lowers to normal, but I'm so ashamed of my reaction that my cheeks are still burning. "I, I'm sorry," I babble as I pull the duvet to my chin. "That wasn't about, you know...."

"No, it's my fault," he says. It's as if he searches my gaze for emotion, as if he's trying to gauge what I'm feeling. "I had to raise your body temperature fast, and I might have overdone it. I was worried about the consequences if I didn't act fast."

That reminds me why I'm here, now that my brain has thawed as well. "Oh, really?" I grunt through my teeth. "But you weren't worried when you had your people push me off the window ledge."

"It was a test you had to take."

I kick my legs in anger, causing him to get up from the bed. I notice that his body had been half bare of his ice-metal armoring, which now starts crawling up his body again, covering his beautiful sinews.

"I didn't have to do anything, you bastard. You pushed me into it."

He cocks an eyebrow. "Watch your language, Lady de Saelaria. Your position has been elevated, but I am still your King."

"Watch my language or what? You almost killed me, twice, I'm not afraid of what you might do to me. *Lysander.*"

He squares his shoulders and lifts his chin, his large shape intimidating. But I'm too angry to stop. I'm no white-knuckling the duvet over my chest.

"Get some rest," he commands, and turns to leave the room. "Your friend will be back with food and drink. Have it all, you need to regain your strength."

"What I need is to know exactly what you intend to do with me now."

He stops in his tracks, but doesn't turn around.

"You better start talking, Milord. Why am I valuable to you, as a descendant of the ocean king? Because forgive me, but I don't believe you just wanted to establish my origins, and that is that."

The door opens, and Edith walks in, balancing a tray of food in her hands that are clearly not used to that kind of work. Pablo manipulates a tray of drinks—I can identify from here water, orange juice, and coffee with milk. My nostrils flare when I sniff the latte.

"Leave it all on her bedside table, and leave," Lysander commands, returning to me. He only movies a hand in the direction of a fancy armchair with silver cushions, and his magic pulls it over.

"Help yourself," he invites as soon as the two have left the chamber, motioning to the rich trays they left on the bedside table, the croissants steaming hot. "It will be a long conversation, and you'll need your attention set on me, not on your grumbling tummy."

CHAPTER IV

Lysander

Arielle keeps the duvet close to her chest with one small hand as she swings her legs over the edge of the bed, and grabs a croissant. She would drop it and hiss under normal circumstances, the croissant is hot, but her body is even hotter now.

I refuse to dwell on why I went so far with her temperature. I felt this undeniable curiosity towards her body, I wanted to explore it. But with every inch I freed from under the duvet, the more I craved to see.

"Start talking," she says. I need a moment to remember what I was supposed to say.

It's strange, how this girl can distract me. What is it about her that makes her so compellingly attractive? Is it the contrast between her shiny black hair and milky skin that's so pleasant to the eye? Or is it those dreamy blue eyes that could drown the onlooker in their mystery? As a fae king I've seen many beautiful women in my life, and many of them have thrown themselves at me. But none of them intrigued me the way this one does.

"The ocean king never intended to have children, or so they say," I begin, leaning back in the armchair.

"I don't know if it's true, because I didn't exist back then. Back when the waters were created, millions of years ago. But when water nymphs appeared, the temptation was too great even for him."

"Water nymphs, are those mermaids?"

"No, mermaids are something else."

"So they're real, too?" There's wonder in her eyes. "Aunt Miriam said they were, but she never actually saw one."

"They're real, but they exist in the supernatural realms, and rarely ever cross into the mortal realm. It did happen a few times, otherwise the stories wouldn't have been born."

"So the ocean king fell in love with a nymph." She takes another bite of the croissant, and a sip of the latte. It's strange, but I like watching her eat.

"He fell in love with a number of them, and had many children. But one of his mistresses was special, and he announced he would make her his queen, which enraged the ocean witch, who had other plans for the ocean people. So she sent word to the ocean king asking for an invitation to his castle, alleging she'd had a vision which she would announce to his subjects, and which would elevate him and his wife-to-be in front of the sea people. The ocean witch was famous, feared and respected in the entire ocean of the Flipside, and having praise come from her was valuable.

"So the king accepted. But what the ocean witch had to say did anything but elevate the king—she prophesized that the child would bring doom to all the ocean's supernatural folk. She did it in such a way, that the merfolk lost their minds, and started a massacre, killing all the king's mistresses, and all the children he had fathered. Any descendant the ocean king might could become a danger to the ocean people, the witch alleged."

She swallows dryly, finally blinking again.

"The pregnant nymph managed to escape, but her only chance was the mortal world. That's where she gave birth to your father, who was a water fae, a hybrid between the ocean king and a water nymph. He returned to the Flipside millions of years later, as the only blood descendant of the ocean king. He was a hunted man ever since then, but he was strong enough to protect himself—until he met your mother, a human, and fell in love. Falling in love weakens people, makes them vulnerable, which made what followed unavoidable. Your father was one of the oldest fae alive, it was a great loss to all the realms when he passed."

"But then..." she whispers, "How about Aunt Miriam, how are we related? She said she was my father's sister."

"That's very possible. Your grandmother had more children later in her life, with other men."

"What about the ocean witch. Is she still alive?"

"Yes."

"And the ocean king?"

"Taken with grief, he cried until his entire being liquefied, turning into sea water. He never fathered other children, and he was never seen in his king shape again. He became one with the ocean. The last thing he ever said was that, since he didn't know where his

66

pregnant bride was hiding, he would be everywhere for her, and the waters would obey her orders wherever she was. Every drop of seawater contains at least an atom of his organic body, and will respond to his descendant's calling. Which brings us to the subject of your powers—as the descendant of the ocean king, every drop of water in the ocean obeys your command. All waters bow to you. I hope you can grasp how huge this is."

"Heaven's sakes," she says, pressing the back of her wrist against her mouth. She stares at me with big eyes, as if peering through the universe's grand design.

I watch her deep blue eyes change as she grasps the power she must have felt when she fell into the ocean's embrace, and her body shifted into water. I watched that process in reverse form the moment she rose on a throne of water to the tower.

"You were impressive to behold," I tell her. "A water queen, made of rippling waves. If you could have seen yourself."

"The way I felt," she whispers. "Like I had access to every mystery of the universe. When my body chemistry changed, it was..." Her voice fades, she's lost for words. I nod.

"I know what it feels like, we all do, at the Winter Court. We're full fae, we can shift, too."

Her eyes slip down my body, and my cock reacts. I stiffen in my seat, refusing to believe that just happened.

"But you can do more than that, can't you?" she says. "More than just transform your body into ice. Your skin can shift into armor."

"It's not just my skin." I clench my jaw to pull myself together. She makes me feel things that worry me. "My whole body changes, on the inside as well. I become insanely difficult to kill, my flesh turns into armor that's almost impossible to pierce."

"Why *almost*?"

"Because there are high fae powerful enough to do it."

"Like who?"

"We weren't talking about me, Lady de Saelaria, we were talking about you."

"What's with the Lady? You called me Arielle before."

"I didn't know who you were. Or I wasn't sure. Now I know for a fact you're a noblewoman."

Her eyes narrow into slits as she gives me the best glare she's capable of.

"It shouldn't matter, you know. Who someone is. Everybody deserves to be treated as if they're important. Pain and suffering feels the same under everyone's skin."

"You have a point, and I completely agree. But when you're a high fae that has to ensure the safety of an entire fae realm, thousands upon thousands of people looking to you for protection, safety, even happiness, you have to make tough choices. You learn that some people need to be more 'equal' than others, simply because sometimes you have to sacrifice one in order to save a hundred. Just put yourself in that situation. What would you do?"

"I don't know, I've never been in your shoes, but I'm pretty sure I wouldn't subject people to the kind of 'test' you put me through. Humans are far younger and baser than fae, and yet they stopped doing shit like that centuries ago."

"Only that test could have revealed your identity. And now that you know the story behind it, you know why it was so enormously important. If you'd failed that test, you could have died, it's true. But the fact that you survived it means you'll save thousands of lives. It was worth the risk. Besides, I would have jumped in for you, if you hadn't come back. I would have saved you."

She crosses her arms over her chest, making a point of how she still doesn't trust me. "Good to know. But how am I saving thousands of lives?"

I clench my jaw, buying time. I'm still trying to figure out how to tell her the truth.

"Like I said, as a descendant of the ocean king you have power over water, in all realms. Power so great it takes a broad consciousness to even grasp it. Imagine it like a sports car with so much horsepower and special inner workings that it takes a formula one pilot to drive it, the average Joe just won't do."

"Sorry to disappoint, but I'm not the average Joe. I'm the average Jane."

"Sorry if I offend you, but it's the truth. You need training before you can fully wield your power. And that's not all. You would need special protection in the supernatural realms. There are many dangerous supernaturals that crave what you have, and that will do anything to get their hands on it. They'd even make a deal with me, give me anything I want in exchange for you."

Moments of silence follow, and I can see in her eyes that she understands.

"So you intend to trade me." She scoffs. "Can't say I didn't expect it would be something like that. Letting me freeze to death in a dungeon, or downing me would have suited you much better, but when you discovered I was special, you had new ideas. Why torment me to death when you can sell me, and get more than just pleasure out of it."

"I would never send you to your death."

"Stop the charade, Lysander. It's just you and me in here, no one else to pretend for. Those supernaturals you're talking about want to kill me, just like they did with the ocean king's other children."

"The ocean witch would want to kill you, yes. Others would want your power, and they can't take it, unless you're very much alive."

"Come on. Aunt Miriam taught me enough about the fae to know that our power cannot simply be taken or given."

"No, but it can be temporarily borrowed."

"What do you mean?"

It's hard to look into her eyes and say this, but here it goes.

"If a man beds you, your powers merge with his. He would then be able to wield your water magic for weeks, the first three days completely and fully. Then the powers would slowly fade."

She jumps to her feet, crimson flush staining her cheeks.

"Are you going to sell me like a, a—?" She can't even say the word, her voice stumbling over it. The silver drawings I put on her light up, undulating on her skin. She seems a beautiful water nymph in silver chains. My cock twitches, the muscles in my thighs stiffen. What the hell?

"You asked for the truth, I'm giving you the truth." Low threat creeps into my tone, which makes her stand down. I've done too much to her already, and she's afraid of me, which hurts. But right now I'm just trying to mask my desire for her. It's unacceptable for me to feel that way about her.

"I brought you in from the human world because you'd used your magic, thereby breaking supernatural law. I was considering punishing your Aunt Miriam for raising you there, since that in itself is forbidden."

"You promised you wouldn't touch Aunt Miriam," she says, glaring at me from under her highly arched eyebrows. "If you do, I will not cooperate."

"I won't harm your Aunt, and not only because I promised you. But because I understand why she raised you there. It was the only safe hiding place." I motion to the food. "Eat, it's getting cold."

"I'm not hungry anymore."

"I can hear your stomach grumble. It's not going to help anybody if you starve to death."

She grabs another croissant, going for the latte with the other hand.

"Tell me, Arielle," I continue. "What stories has your Aunt Miriam told you about your parents?"

"She did tell me that they were killed, assassinated, so I know that much," she says. "And she told me it wasn't safe for me in the supernatural realms."

"Did she ever tell you who killed your parents, and why?"

Tears sparkle in her dreamy blue eyes that keep me captivated in a way that nothing ever has. It's hard to keep my focus, and not let my thoughts stray to how she would look completely naked. Must be her mermaid powers doing this to me. Even though my magic keeps them at a minimum, suppressed, they're natural to her, and seep to the surface.

"They were assassinated on sight, under the accusation of treason. It was a fabricated accusation."

I nod. "That's the information I have, too."

I already know her story, but I sit quietly and allow her to tell it. I can see that it helps her release some of her frustration.

"Like you said, my father had moved back to the Flipside, but he would often go on missions in the human world. He knew the human world extremely well, having lived in it for thousands of years, so the Council of the Arcane charged him with tracking down fae, demons and other creatures of darkness that would seek to prey on humans, and form entire mobs. But someone framed him, and made it look like he was working with those gangs. They executed him on sight. Then they tracked down my mother, and assassinated her, simply because she knew about the supernatural, and she was a liability."

My jaw clenches. "You were unjustly orphaned, and I want you to know I'm sorry about that. You were only a baby, you still needed them so much."

"How do you know I was a baby?"

"I told you, I have information. The version that has been brought to my knowledge is very similar to yours. No need to go into details."

"Okay, so I'm the ocean king's descendant, and I have power over the ocean—power I can't feel anymore, because of the limitations you put on me." She looks demonstratively at the silver drawings on her arms. "And now you intend to sell me to the highest bidder, am I right? I suppose you'll also try to get the best deal for my virginity."

Wait, what?.

"You're... You never?"

She raises an eyebrow. "I'm half fae. I have the fae trait that I only feel lust when I'm in love, and I've only been in love once. Unrequited. So here I am."

I can't help scanning her up and down. It feels like I'm undressing her with my eyes, and by the way she wraps the duvet around herself, she feels it, too.

"Let's just say it's unusual to meet someone from the mortal world who is a virgin at twenty-two. But you're right, being half fae... So you were in love once?" Now why am I hung up on that?

"I don't want to talk about it," she murmurs, looking down. That heats me up. An uncomfortable feeling grips my throat.

"You still have feelings for him?"

"I said, I don't want to talk about it."

"I'm afraid you'll have to." I rise from the chair. She stares up at me from the bed, and the way her eyes land on me, long black lashes hooding them, it makes my blood boil. Get a grip, Lysander, you're the fucking Winter King.

"Your Aunt Miriam hid you from the supernatural world because she feared for your life," I explain. "She relinquished her fae looks and aged as a human, because she needed all the camouflage she could get. She knew powerful supernaturals were after you, and any man who ever entered your life could have been a spy for them."

"Well, it's pretty obvious my first love wasn't one. I'm here, in your power, not some other guy's that might have sent him."

Silence falls between us.

"Lysander, I'd like one thing to be clear as day between us," she says, standing up and squaring her shoulders, holding the duvet above her breasts. "I may be forced to let you handle my body like merchandise, chained and powerless as you sell me to the highest bidder. But my secrets are my own, like my soul."

She defies me with those eyes. So much smaller than me, barely more than a girl, and yet so much power inside her. I can feel her magic rippling in her core with her anger. The lure of a mermaid coils around her, as fine as morning fog. I wonder—if she were to sing now, would I be able to resist her?

I can feel lust bubbling up inside of me, which can only mean one thing. A thing I'm not prepared to accept, or to deal with.

I step back, ready to go.

"Catch some sleep. We're leaving soon, you'll need all your strength."

"Leaving where?"

"To meet the 'highest bidder'." My lips curl as the words roll off my tongue, leaving a bitter taste behind.

"I see," she hisses. Her blue eyes fill with resentment, and I can't believe how wretched that makes me feel. "I must say, you're a great disappointment, Lord of Winter. For someone as ancient and powerful as you, as experienced and wise, you're nothing more than a medieval inquisitor. You subject me to a deadly test as if you were on a witch hunt, and now you want to trade me over to some guy." She sticks out her chin, arms folded in defiance across her chest. "And what if I refuse? What if I tell your 'highest bidder' to go to hell?"

I hate it, but I have to do this. My jaw ticks. "You won't, if you care about your Aunt Miriam's safety."

Her cheeks go deep crimson with anger, but she doesn't say anything.

"The problems might extend to your new friend Edith Snowstorm, too."

"You would harm two innocent people if I don't fuck who you tell me to?" she growls.

I just stare at her, which she takes as answer enough.

"Now I understand how you've stayed king of the Winter Realm for so many years. You're a tyrant, a bully, you would sell your own mother if it brought you what you wanted."

"Everything I do is for the greater good."

"Yeah, sure."

We stare hard at each other, her arms locked over her chest, her face red. It hurts to see the hatred in her eyes, which I wish would look upon me with... Damn it, I want her to crave me.

"The humans have a saying, Lord of Winter," she says, almost like a curse. "People always meet twice in life. When we meet for the second time, I'll make you pay for this."

It's a threat, and yet it has a soothing effect on me—it's a promise that we will meet again.

"Now do me the honor of leaving my chamber," she demands, turning her back to me. I still stand rooted in the ground, watching her black hair fall over her shoulders like rivulets of liquid ebony. It caresses the milky skin of her back, the duvet draped over her loins. She's sobbing lightly, I can tell by the way her shoulder blades move.

"Now," she says in a cracked voice. I walk slowly backwards, eyes still on her, fighting an overwhelming need to stay with her.

Once the door is closed behind me, I start down the hallway at a rapid pace, trying to break this thread that ties me to her. I can feel the guards staring after me. They've never seen me like this before, and frankly, I don't recognize myself either. There's only one place that I can go to now, and I head straight for it.

⁂

Lysander

"WHAT IN THE CURSED realms is wrong with you?" Sandros grunts.

I'm pacing his room like an angry lion. His chamber is spacious, but also Spartan, since he is a true military man. I head to one of the archways that face the ocean, gripping the ledge.

"Fuck this," I hiss.

"Are you gonna tell me what 'this' is all about?"

I look at him over my shoulder. He stands there bare-chested, black pants on. He just got out of a bath, his long hair damp, a plain white shirt in his hand.

"I'm sorry, I needed to..." What am I going to say, that I've fallen prey to the charms of a water nymph?

He frowns at me. "Is this about the water princess?"

"Arielle, yes. I just told her what's going to happen with her next."

"And how did she take it?"

"How do you think?"

He doesn't say it. It's understood.

"I have to admit, I feel sorry for her," he says.

"I do, too."

Sandros slides his shirt on, leaving it open and removing his silver dagger from the sheath on his bedside table. He walks over as he polishes it.

"I have a team of military messengers teleporting to Xerxes," he says. "I expect them to be back by morning."

"Fine. Keep the portal open the whole time, so they can return easily, but have soldiers in place in case they bring back more than just themselves from the Fire Realm."

"They call it Purgatory these days."

"Yeah, I keep forgetting." I stare out at the ocean, allowing the sundown to mirror in my eyes. "I wouldn't put it beyond Xerxes to take advantage of the messenger portal, and use it to attack. He's as treacherous as Lucifer."

"But sadly not as pretty." The sound of stone polishing metal fills the air between us as we stand side by side, watching the sunset. We've bonded over stuff like this for ages. My little brother, and weapons, I feel most at home with them.

"So, tell me about the girl," he begins as the mood loosens. "What happened that made you barge in here looking like a madman?"

"I don't know, it's just... I feel things I shouldn't fucking feel."

Sandros laughs.

"What's so funny?"

"First of all, you're swearing. You never swear. The girl is messing with your head, and she can't even tap into her full powers."

"Messing with my head." I stare out at the dying sun, its orange rays spreading like thinned blood over the horizon. "I'll have to start using protection against her charms, the same way as the sailor fae of old did."

"You're not really considering amulets, are you? You're the fucking Lord of Winter, King of the Winter Realm, the feared and respected Lysander Nightfrost. Mermaids and water nymphs got nothing on you."

"This one does."

"Strange. You've got natural shields against all kinds of magic. Only higher fae and divine supernaturals from the highest realms can drill through them."

"Arielle de Saelaria isn't just anyone either. She is the ocean king's descendant."

"But her magic is under control, isn't it? You put a silver spell on her."

"What if it isn't her magic that's doing this? What if it's...her nature, something that's as much a part of her as her eyes?"

"You mean you feel naturally attracted to her? Because if that's the case, it's simple—just take her; she's your prisoner, you have the right to subdue her sexually." He shrugs, still polishing his blade. "You'd be doing her a favor anyway. I doubt Xerxes will be concerned with her pleasure. In fact, he might enjoy hurting her while he takes her."

My jaw clenches so hard it hurts. "Especially when he learns that she's a virgin."

"Say what?" He angles his body to me, his interest piqued. "But she's twenty-two, lived in the mortal realm. How can she still be a virgin in a world where girls—"

"Apparently she's taking physical intimacy very seriously. Or she's frigid, I don't know. But it seems she's special in more ways than we originally thought."

"Fuck me."

"I feel guilty for what's going to happen to her," I continue quietly. "Xerxes will surely marry her, tie her to him permanently. He'll take her again and again in order to renew his power over her domain, and no one will be able to save her once they're officially mated."

A vision fills my mind of Xerxes parting the girl's legs at the wedding, his golden body glowing in the low light of candles, as the white folds of her bride gown flow like a cascade from the edges of the bed.

"All the more reason for you to be her first," Sandros says. "And make sure she has an

79

unforgettable experience. That way the poor thing will get at least a taste of what sensuality should feel like. With a little luck, in time, she might even guide Xerxes in the right direction."

"I don't think Xerxes wants to be guided. Her pleasure will never interest him. Better for her not to know what she's missing out on. She would have to live with more than just the pain and disgust of being with that monster, she'd be full of frustration and regret, too. Besides, Xerxes could use my having taken her first as a pretext not to honor the blood bond we'll make. The magic world allows that, if one of the parties genuinely feels betrayed."

Sandros frowns his dark eyebrows. "Yeah, about that. Do we even know how to make a blood bond?"

"Our officers for Lore and Ancient History do. Edith Snowstorm's family."

"We'll need more than that to—"

"Relax, I have a plan." I pause, contemplating the situation. "I'd never do this without one. We're standing at a vital crossroads in the history of all realms. This cold war between fire and winter fae has been going on for so long, and has been so bloody, that the chance of ending it is priceless." I look into my half-brother's eyes. "We can't risk anything going wrong, Sandros."

"So you're basically sacrificing the girl, fully aware that she's going to live a life of hell with Xerxes."

My lips press in a hard line, but I have to look the truth in the face.

"If this were only about me alone, Sandros, I'd rather fight Xerxes to death than put the girl through this. But thousands upon thousands of fae lives depend on this. So many are dying every day in this war over supremacy." I stare out at the ocean as the final sunrays drown into the horizon.

Arielle

"THIS IS OUTRAGEOUS, sick, unacceptable," I snap as I pace my chamber. I hitch up the folds of my pale blue dress, and drop them angrily. "He's not only selling me to the highest bidder, he has me dress up like a courtesan, too."

Edith stares at me from the bed where she's sitting with her legs tucked under her. The tense look in her otherwise soft brown eyes tells me she just wants me to calm down, I'm making her nervous.

I turn to the vanity table mirror, trying hard to keep back the swear words pooling in my mouth. I'm wearing a pompous dress with a corset that Edith helped tighten around my body, because Xerxes likes seeing women's bare shoulders, especially when they're delicate, like mine—or so Minerva relayed to us through Pablo, when she sent the dress. Also, she'd forwarded the order that my breasts should display a 'nice swell', without a necklace to soften the impact.

"I look like a—" I want to say prostitute, but clench my teeth on time. Pablo has just appeared in the door.

"Everything is set, Milady," he says. "We're leaving."

81

Another reason why I could spit Lysander in the face. The man seems set on going from wrong to wronger every freaking day. That he sells me, and puts my life in danger, is one thing, but he also insisted that Edith and Pablo came along as my own small retinue, to mark my status as a noble fae.

I square my shoulders, and wait for Edith to join me before starting to the door. The guards wait for us to pass them, then I hear them marching behind us, their metallic footwear clamoring against the castle floor. By the time we reach the ground floor, where we can hear the ocean waves crashing against the castle's rocky base, a small army has gathered behind us.

In the middle of the main hall we meet three other small armies—Minerva with her people to the left, her predator eyes fixed on me; Sandros with his military squad of fae in silver and metal to the right, and Lysander right in front of me in all his splendor. He's wearing mailed armor that hugs his muscular body in a way that would make any woman drool, his shiny golden hair flowing to his broad shoulders, his chiseled warrior-king features set in grim determination.

Something stirs in my core when I look at him, but force myself to keep my wits about me. I clench my fists, hiding them behind my back, making sure that he can't see that I'm struggling. I have to stop ogling Lysander, or he'll realize that I have an urge to touch his body. It looks indestructible, and I can't help wondering what it would feel like on me.

He takes a step forward, his men slamming their heels into the ground. It reverberates against the castle walls with the sound of war.

"As we expected, Xerxes has asked for a meeting, so he can see the ocean king's descendant with his own eyes."

I notice more fae noblemen appearing on the winding stairs that glow with icicles and magic, heads leaning over the ivory banister at the upper levels.

"The meeting will take place on neutral ground," he continues, his powerful voice filling the hall, traveling upward to the gathering on the stairs. "The Flipside won't do in this case. The danger of either of us having hidden allies is too great—his argument, not mine."

"I know where this is going, and it's unacceptable," one of the gathered noblemen puts in. "We punish people for crossing those borders, we can't break the rules ourselves. If crossing over becomes an option, many will find ways to take it." I recognize him as one of the older fae from the Council, leaning on an ivory cane, bright magic coiling around it. Aunt Miriam told me about it, it's the sort of magic that comes only with exquisite wisdom.

"It was Xerxes' request, and I accepted," Lysander replies. "I can't back out of it anymore, Iridion. Besides, this will be a highly secured meeting, it will not meddle much with the human world. It's taking place at sea." His ice-blue eyes find mine. Damn it, why does my heart jump like this every time he looks at me? He is a villain, and I must resent him.

"What do you mean at sea?" old Iridion inquires.

"We're meeting in the middle of the ocean," he says. "It's the safest thing to do, since we're using the ocean as a portal. We dive in on the Flipside, and emerge in the mortal world at the spot where we're supposed to meet. We come back the same way. With so much water around, Xerxes won't have fire to draw on and hi-jack this."

"It's all well-thought of," Sandros adds.

"Be careful, Milord," Iridion warns. "I'm afraid you're underestimating Xerxes. He's known for his cunning. If he agreed to this, he might have an ace up in his sleeve."

Lysander smiles. "So do I."

People murmur. My eyes fly to Minerva, whose gaze is charged with lust. My teeth crunch.

Lysander walks closer to me, drawing my attention back to him. "Before you hate on me too hard for this dress," he says low enough that only I can hear him, "Let me tell you it's special. Once inside the water, you'll see."

Lysander signals two of the servants, and they come forth with clothes for Edith and Pablo. They bend their heads and stretch out both arms, offering the outfits to the sweet winter fae and the nerdy servant boy. The clothes are pale blue, the same color as my dress, but far less pretentious.

"Put them on, so that you can withstand the portal. The ocean can be vicious."

The two servants accompany Edith and Pablo to a side room, where they can change. I look down at my dress. It's got pretty folds that resemble sea waves, and the corset is made of a fabric that feels like satin. It's beautiful, and it showcases the shape of my body nicely. At least I think it does, considering the way Lysander looks at me. It sends thrills down my spine.

"All right then," Minerva raises her voice. "I will have the rescue squad ready. At the first sign you need us, we're jumping into the portal."

I stare at the army behind her. "You'd be bringing *all* of them?"

She stares me up and down like I'm beneath her. "The half-breed still underestimates supernatural power. She clearly thinks such a squad unnecessarily large and too heavily armed for the occasion. But maybe it's better that way. If she did understand the complete scope of the threat she's facing, she'd probably go mad."

"I'm sure if I'd been given the chance to grow up in the supernatural world, I would have better knowledge of that scope. But unfortunately my family had to hide me away from supernaturals in order to keep me around, and breathing."

Giggles ripple all around. A fae whispers, "she told her," somewhere close. Waves of pleasant emotion touch my skin—not my own, but that of fae that actually start to like me simply for having defied this bitch. I can't help but glance at Lysander, too curious for his reaction. I think I see a small smile in the corner of his beautiful mouth, but it might be just wishful thinking.

Crimson stains Minerva's cheeks. She raises her sharp chin like a banshee, her thin lips sucking lemon until her mouth pulls into a dark red pucker. When she

85

unclenches her jaw to say something, she doesn't get the chance to. Edith and Pablo re-emerge, Edith in a simple, pale-blue dress, and Pablo in a suit. He is pleasant to the eye with his ashen hair and intelligent young features, and now that I see him dressed smartly, I notice he moves with almost the same grace as Edith.

"We're meeting Xerxes on a cruise ship, the Belinda," Lysander says. "We'll use the ocean as portal, and when we emerge on the other side, we'll swim to it."

He faces me, as well as Edith and Pablo who flank me on each side.

"When we emerge into the mortal world," he says, "we'll have to find a way into the ship from underneath. We can't risk anybody seeing us, whether crew or tourists. Since none of you three has experience with the ocean as a portal, you'll need support. Edith goes with Sandros." She petrifies when she hears it. One glance at Lysander's half-brother is enough to understand why. Big, with his wild dark hair and those demonic golden eyes, he could drive chills into anyone, especially someone as delicate as Edith. "Pablo will go with Eldan, Sandros' best soldier." That's the man on his right, a white-haired, sharp-eyed and hawk-nosed fae. "You, princess of the ocean, will go with me."

My head snaps to him, my heart stopping. I stare at the beautiful king in his ice-metal mail that hugs his powerful body.

"No, you can't burden yourself with that," Minerva reacts, but I can hear the jealousy in her tone. "You're the king, you're far too important, you cannot risk—"

"The most important person now is Arielle," he cuts her off, his eyes cold and sharp.

He holds out his hand for me, which has taken the form of a gauntlet. The moment my fingers touch the metal, a jolt goes through me. It's cold, and so sleek it's hard to believe that it's organic. And yet it is, I know it.

I walk next to him, and I can't help thinking he does it as if he's taking me to the altar. He holds my gaze the entire time, and warmth rises inside of me, turning into heat. I bite my lower lip, afraid this is arousal, and he's going to see it.

"Relax," he says quietly. "Let me adjust your body temperature. It might get icy down there."

He leads me to a huge archway opening to the ocean, presiding over all the others. My teeth start to chatter. I'm filled with both excitement and fear. When I think we're going to step onto that ledge, and look down at the waves crashing against the rocks at the bottom... Luckily, Lysander understands perfectly what I'm going through.

He holds my hand as I step onto the ledge. My heart beats in my throat, and my blood pressure must have sky-rocketed. My vision blurs as I look down at the wild foamy waves that now rise higher, as if reaching for me, wanting to pull me down into them.

"Don't be afraid," Lysander says as he steps onto the ledge by my side. "Don't focus on what we're about to do, focus on the warmth in your body."

I move my attention from the threatening ocean to the rising heat in my core, realizing it's Lysander that's causing it.

I look at him from the corner of my eye, his golden hair floating like silk around his head, his chiseled profile so beautiful that it hurts. The sharp lines of his cheekbones, the strong contour of his jaw, his skin that seems made of snow and ice, the bastard is magnificent. He could be so easy to love, if he weren't a villain.

My eyes rest on his beautiful lips, sensual and yet with a strong, manly contour. I let his beauty pull me in, distract me from the awareness of what we're about to do. And as I let it pervade me, I become aware of something else—Minerva's glare stabbing my back, poisoned with jealousy.

"Just remember one thing," Lysander says. "Before we hit the water, take a deep breath."

A thought starts to form in my head, but Lysander jumps into the waves with me, and my mind goes blank.

I swear this moment falling down into the waves, hand in hand with Lysander, is the longest moment that ever existed in time. I cry out, a long sharp scream as my hair whips around me, the folds of my dress flapping loudly. The wind presses against my nostrils, making it impossible to breathe. The water races closer to my feet, and I manage to pull myself together enough to swallow a deep breath in the last second.

Our legs pierce the water, a high wave curling over us, pushing us under. Powerful currents pull at my feet, and my hand slips from Lysander's sleek metallic grip. I scream No, bubbles leaving my mouth as the current pulls me under.

The dress begins transforming, crawling on my body like a second skin, to the point that it's almost painful. It makes close contact with my body, squeezing the water off of me. I've lost the breath of air I've taken when I screamed, and I flail desperately, when I see Lysander's face swimming to me, his golden hair floating around him.

When he's close he wraps his metallic arms around me, and pulls me into a kiss. Time stops as I blink under water, feeling those perfectly contoured lips on mine. When he parts them and blows air into my mouth, I understand what he's doing. I run my arms around his neck, and hold on to him as he swims downward, towards the dark depths of the ocean.

He unlocks himself from me, but holds my hand, which is now covered up to my fingertips in what seems like pale blue scales. The deeper we go the more the light fades, and the water pressure weighs heavier, pressing down on my back.

It's amazing, experiencing the ocean like this. One by one colorful lights appear, adorning the darkness like stars in the sky, in colorful shapes so beautiful I forget what I'm doing here. It feels like I can touch galaxies in skies made of liquid void. I think about water predators, and whether or not they'd be dangerous to us, but I think we've been moving too fast for that. The pressure is now too much, but when I think I can't take it anymore it just stops, and decreases as if time moves in reverse.

The heat inside my body keeps me connected to Lysander, in a way that makes us part of each other. I realize that I feel him inside me in an almost sexual way. His face, his hair, and his entire body are glowing, gold and ice and steel. A feeling of joy envelops me, a feeling that things are just as they're supposed to be. The feeling is so strong and so pleasant that I stop kicking the water.

But something hits me from behind. I turn to look, but can't see more than a whirl through the dark water. To my surprise, it seems we're leaving it, and not heading toward it. Light starts to filter through the waves again like daylight through lace curtains. A school of fish races past us, creating a vacuum that pushes us back, but Lysander pulls me forward.

Soon I can see the surface rippling above my eyes. I emerge out of the water, drawing one deep breath. I tread the water, looking around. My wet hair clings to my forehead and my face, but I can still see Lysander, his hair glowing in the sunlight. His brother shoots up from the water, too, along with Edith, and Eldan with Pablo.

There's only water as far as I can see, but Lysander points to something in the distance. His arm is now only corded muscle, white and glistening with seawater, without the metal and ice layers.

"There," he says.

We all look in the direction he pointed, and spot a cruise ship. It's far enough that it seems small, but close enough that I can make out its shape.

As we swim towards the ship I wonder when we hit the bottom of the ocean. It all happened too fast, but I would have noticed if we'd hit solid ground. And I'm sure we never did. I make a mental note to ask Lysander if that's how water portals work.

Cold starts to seep into my body. I remember it's around Christmas time here in the mortal world.

"God, it's freezing," I say to Lysander, my teeth chattering. He reaches over and winds an arm around my waist, pulling me to his side. He's completely naked in the water, his body white and shining beautifully like snow in the moonlight.

"Why is it colder than on the Flipside?"

"It's not, but the connection between us ripped when we emerged at the surface. That connection was what kept you warm."

As he drives warmth into my body, a Christmas tree adorned with lights becomes visible on the highest deck at the ship's rear.

"I can't believe it," I whisper. "You arrested me from the mortal world in November, and it's already been a month. It seemed like days to me."

"Your confusion is normal, one can lose track of time in supernatural realms," Lysander says as he swims towards the ship.

"Sure, especially when one goes through hell there," I sting him.

"Now. Dive and follow me," he says.

I can hear the air fill the others' lungs as they pull in a deep breath. Lysander holds me firmly by my waist with one arm.

"Ready?"

I breathe in deeply, and nod. We dive in, hand in hand. He leads us under the ship.

The feeling is glorious, and overwhelming at the same time. Just imagine seeing the underbelly of the Titanic floating above you. It's so close that the propellers could cut us to pieces. But they move slowly under water compared to our speed as Lysander pushes through the whirls they form. When we're at the middle of the ship we swim sideways, rising to the surface.

Just a little above water level there's a hatch.

"We have to move quickly," Lysander says as the others join us. We form a tight cluster now, plastered to the ship's side so nobody can see us. "If the ship tilts only a little it would be enough for water to seep in through the hatch, and the alarms would go off. We don't want that kind of attention, it would lead to our discovery, so we have to move fast."

He places his big hand on the hatch, closes his eyes, and murmurs a spell. White magic crackles under his palm, and spreads to the rest of the hatch.

The hatch hisses as it unsticks from its seals. Lysander's fingers slip underneath, and he opens it. He helps me up first, and then slides in quickly like a sea snake. Sandros pushes Edith up by her waist, and follows. Eldan helps Pablo up, but when he hoists himself on his hands, the ship tilts.

It's just a little, probably a slight change of direction since ships don't move like cars, but enough for water to slip inside. And enough for the sensor to light up red, and set off the alarm.

A sharp ring pierces my ears, causing me to press my hands to the sides of my head. I can hear Sandros call Eldan's name, and I see the latter slipped back into the water. Lysander and Sandros both reach after him to pull him back up.

"Hurry," I call. "I can hear steps on the deck just above us, and they're moving fast."

But a current has taken hold of Eldan. Lysander jumps into the water for him, and it takes only seconds until he swims with the man back to the ship, but the alarm is now so loud there's no way they won't find us.

Lysander pushes himself back up, his triceps cording up. As soon as he's in again, we start running.

"We're dripping water," Sandros says behind us. "They'll realize someone slipped inside, and they'll follow our trail."

Lysander scoops me up in his arms as we run. "I'm going to drive my body temperature into you, and I'll do it fast, so whatever you feel, don't panic."

"Is that how you did it all along," I breathe. "You channeled your body heat into me?"

"I am the Lord of Winter, let's say I have body warmth to spare. I'm comfortable at the lowest temperatures, and turning cold as ice also stops the dripping."

"How about the others, what will they do?"

"They're all winter fae, they can cool down, like me. Sandros can up his body temperature, too."

So the rumor that he's part fire fae must be true.

Lysander's body heat pours into me as he speaks, until the water suit starts taking the form of a dress around me, now that all the humidity is gone. Even my hair dries in a matter of seconds.

He maneuvers me through narrow white corridors that look much more modern than in the movie Titanic, which is pretty much all I've seen of cruise ships. It all went down too fast for me to know which turns we took, but I'm a little dizzy when Lysander puts me down in a narrow corridor. I become instantly aware of how I'd been pressed to his naked body. By the time I look down, his flesh has transformed into what looks like liquid metal where pants should be.

We walk into what seems to be the crew cabins deck.

"Wait here," Lysander says, and slips through a side door. He returns within mere seconds with clothes."

"We'll need to blend in," he says.

I couldn't agree more, because I don't see how any of the men could pass for human in their liquid metal armors. Not to mention their beauty, and the pointy ears, but I guess for those one could find explanations.

We follow the service stairs up to the first class deck.

"Do we *have* to do luxury now?" Sandros mutters behind us.

"The rich are fewer and far between. It's lonelier and more private among them. Not to mention that they're more likely to blame our looks on good plastic surgery."

"What are we waiting for, why aren't we walking?" Edith whispers, glancing worried behind her.

"Shhhh." Lysander narrows his eyes. They emit light as he focuses. "Not all the cabins are taken by the sound of them." He pushes me back, down the coiling stairs and into an alcove on the landing. We cram in there, but he and Sandros are too big, so they have to stay on the landing, which means we have to move extra fast again. Lysander starts to hand out clothes.

"Quickly. Someone might appear any second on the corridor."

The fae shuffle into their clothes with a speed and ease I wouldn't be capable of. I realize I'm the only one who's half human between them, but before I get to dwell on it, Lysander has already taken my hand and started down the narrow corridor. The stolen slacks are too tight on his thighs, and the white shirt on his chest, but it doesn't matter. He seems a beautiful prince on steroids, and it's no wonder the first people that happen in our way stare at him.

He stops abruptly in front of a cabin door, listening for sounds inside.

"This one is empty," he says. "There's no human energy in."

He touches the door and whispers an unlocking spell, which makes the door spring softly from its lock. We slip inside, Edith slapping her back against the door once it's closed, and sliding to the ground.

"God," she breathes in relief. "I was convinced they'd fucking catch us."

Lysander stands in the middle of the room, unmoving, feeling the ship for Xerxes.

I look around for water, my body exhausted from the experience in the ocean. There's a small liquor bar in a corner of the small living room. We're in a small first class suite, with shiny wood-paneling, a wardrobe with mirror doors, a master bed fitting perfectly in an alcove, and a small living room to my right.

I find a bottle of Pellegrino and down it, when I hear Lysander speak.

"I've found him." His voice is powerful, but his eyes fixed on a distant target.

"You've tracked Xerxes' energy?" Sandros says, a frown on his serious face.

"He's up in the saloon." His eyes focus out the window, on the ocean.

Reddish sunset rays have already started to kiss the horizon, spreading over the waves. When I look back at Lysander I jump back. I didn't notice that he'd moved so close to me.

"This is it, Arielle," he says. "This is where you meet your destiny."

"But you're not—" I stutter, stepping back and bracing myself. "You're not gonna hand me over now, are you? I mean, we're only here so that he can meet me, see for himself that I exist, maybe test my magic."

"He won't have you until he and I have taken a blood oath, something we can't do aboard the ship." He looks at me like there's something more I should know, but he's wary of saying it.

"Tell me the truth, Lysander," I whisper, only for him and me. "You expect things to get ugly?"

"All I can tell you is this—if things get ugly, remember why you're doing it. Think of your Aunt Miriam, and Edith."

My jaw tightens, and I remember why I should hate the Lord of Winter.

"Lysander Nightfrost," I murmur. "You make a girl's head spin with your magic when you drive heat inside her, with the way you seem to protect her when she needs it. But the truth is you're a monster. All you care about is your own agenda, and you don't care who you sacrifice for it, or what you put people through."

"Arielle—"

"Just tell me one thing. Tell me if I'm wrong when I say you're giving me over to a man who will mistreat and abuse me. A man that will rape me, repeatedly, and drain my power from me that way. He might keep me in a dark dungeon for ages, for all you know, and use me for sex and power."

His jaw sets. I snort.

"That's what I thought."

CHAPTER V

Lysander

Her words send blades through my heart, slicing a piece of it with every sentence. I can't even look into her pretty face anymore, I can't take the look of betrayal.

"Milord," Eldan's voice pulls me back. "I'm sensing something. It's magic, but a strange kind."

"Maybe Xerxes' squad, tucked hidden somewhere?" Sandros steps in.

"No, that's not what I'm picking up. It's something different, something...exceptional."

My senses spike. I flex them to track down the magic.

"I don't feel warriors. And Xerxes would have been mad to bring them. He wouldn't break the rules of our meeting that way, he knows there's no idea if he does. But I do sense something special, too."

"Xerxes is known for his cunning, brother. What if he's luring us into a trap?" Sandros warns. "He was allowed to bring a retinue, like you brought us, what if they have special powers that can create an ambush?"

I shake my head. "Wouldn't make sense. That would only end in an open battle, and he knows it."

"And don't forget about the Lord Protector, the Grim Reaper," Eldan tells Sandros. "He'd take us all down to the underworld before we could reveal ourselves to the mortals. A battle is out of the question."

"Then what's this magic that we're feeling?" Eldan presses. "Because it sure as hell is something."

"Maybe we should call this off," Sandros says, stepping protectively by Arielle's side.

"No way we're backing down now," Arielle reacts, surprising us all. She balls her small fists at her sides, her bare chest flushing. "I'm not going through this again and again until you get it right." Her blue eyes pierce mine. "But you would enjoy prolonging this, wouldn't you, Lysander? You know damn well this is torture for me, being brought here for a slave master to assess my worth like I'm merchandise. Knowing that he'll do things to me, repeatedly and most probably violently, for the rest of my life—which is bound to be long, as a half fae. To top that, you chained my powers, making it impossible for me to protect myself." She holds a finger in my face. "We're going through with this, Lysander Nightfrost. I want to put this torturous anticipation behind me once and for all. And I hope that every time you admire a sunset over the free ocean, you think of me, and everything you robbed me of."

With tears in her eyes, she runs into the bathroom and slams the door. If she only knew that she's leaving me frayed on the inside. The others are looking at me with curious eyes, especially Sandros. If he only knew what I'm going through.

"I want to help you, brother," he says, placing a hand on my shoulder. "But I really don't know how."

"You can't help me," I reply in a low voice. "No one can."

I leave the suite, seeking solitude and a clear head out on the deck. I take a deep breath, leaning over the banister. For the first time in forever, I probe my feelings. Why do I feel so wretched? What is it that I really want from the water princess?

And it comes to me—I want to be alone with Arielle. I want to have her for myself tonight. Take her to dinner, surround her with flowers, watch her smell the roses. I want to watch her voluptuous breasts moving up and down as she heaves for me. Watch those sweet red lips move as she tells me she wants me.

Fuck, Lysander, snap out of it. You can't be this attracted to the girl, it's forbidden.

"Lysander."

My skin crawls, and my upper lip curls over my teeth. I know that voice.

Arielle

I'LL FINALLY MEET XERXES Blazeborn. My heart slams like crazy in my chest, but I'll be damned if I'll show it.

"Please, by the holy realms, put on a friendly face," Edith pleads as she hovers around with spells of beauty on her hands. I sit at the vanity table, staring at myself in the mirror with a blank expression. "Xerxes can treat you like a slave, or like a queen, and it all depends on how much he's going to like you." She

100

brings her charmed palms close to my cheeks, but I grab them gently and push them down.

"No offense, but I can't believe that a fae can think like this. You're supposed to be far wiser than humans, and yet here you are, advising me to accept that I'm being sold, and make the best of it."

"It's because she is wise that Edith advises you this," Sandros says. He walks closer with his hands pushed into the pockets of his slacks. He seems out of place with his long, wild hair, the shadowy stubble and demonic golden eyes, yet dressed in a starched shirt and slacks. It's like putting a god in plain human clothes. There's no way he won't draw attention in the dining room, just like his brother.

He hunkers down by my side so we can talk at the same level.

"There's no way around this, and you know it, Arielle. The only solution for you is to make the best of this situation. You can be forced to put up with Xerxes' endless abuse, or you could turn the tables in your favor. Why would you refuse to do that? Simply out of principle?"

"Xerxes and others like him—" Meaning Lysander, "—are used to being worshipped and feared, and they won't learn any different unless someone finally stands up to them."

Sandros bursts into laughter, which takes me aback. "Do you honestly think no one has tried in thousands upon thousands of years?" He laughs harder, and Edith, Eldan and Pablo smile, too. They clearly share his opinion.

"It's your call, daughter of the ocean," Sandros says, placing his big hands on his knees and getting up to his feet. "But think about it—is it worth risking all that abuse only to try and teach a thousands-year-old fae a lesson? I for one would play my cards very carefully."

I hate it, but I see that he's right. I square my shoulders, staring at myself in the vanity mirror. Edith applies some of her magic to my face, basically photo-shopping me, since I'm pallid from the journey through the ocean, and from the emotional exhaustion. I see myself change in the mirror like a enchanted portrait. Edith gives me back my Snow White look, my long straight hair falling over my bare shoulders and chest, strands like liquid ebony flowing in rivers over the swell of my breasts. Long black lashes enhance the blue of my eyes, and my lips plump up, red like roses.

"There," Edith says with a smile, pressing her cheek to mine, her kind chocolate eyes meeting mine in the mirror. "You look absolutely dashing, doll."

"Oh God, Edith, you sound so old right now." We both laugh, and I feel my spirits lift. Indeed, not all is lost. I might still find a way to tame my destiny.

"It's time," Sandros says, appearing behind us in the mirror.

We start towards the first class saloon. We meet people, many eyes following us, which makes me restless.

It's not like I'm not used to the attention; being a half-fae in the mortal world sets you apart, but I was never as strikingly fae as I am now.

102

"I hope we get this over with soon," Pablo whispers in my ear. He and Edith walk right behind me, Sandros and Eldan trailing us like royal guards. "We won't be able to stay under the radar for long. We draw attention, the crew will start digging, especially since what happened with the hatch and the alarm."

A hostess greets us with a guest list and a fake smile, but Sandros steps forward and uses a spell to soften her. She offers to find us a table, completely taken with him, but he thanks her and points to Lysander, who's waiting for us on the other side of the saloon.

"We're meeting someone, he's already here," he says, flashing a smile at her, which earns him a groan and rolling eyes from Edith.

We head towards Lysander, his eyes locked on me the whole time. The closer I get, the more my core tightens, and my palms sweat.

Then Lysander moves out of my sight, and the Lord of Fire takes up my field of vision.

Arielle

THE MAN IS AS LARGE as Lysander, and he seems to exude shadow. He's an impressive fae, like Lysander and his brother, which marks him as higher fae. Coal black hair that touches his shoulders, eyes red like fire. He's got lips so red they're almost black, and his skin gives out a golden glow.

"OMG, he's beautiful," Edith gasps behind me.

"He's terrible," Pablo whispers in awe.

He's beautiful in a disturbing kind of way but, in my eyes, he's got nothing on Lysander. I secretly harbored the hope that I might feel attracted to the Lord of Fire, since I'm going to spend the rest of my life with him, and also because I'd love to see Lysander eating his heart out. But damn. He'll never stir me in the ways Lysander does, I know that immediately.

The large fae is equally unimpressed by me, I can tell from the way he looks at me. He gives me a once-over that seems to tell him everything he needs to know, and I think he finds me disappointing. My spirits sink, because I feel deeply things won't go well between us.

He turns on his heel, and heads to a table where his men wait, his sleek suit hugging his athletic back. Edith and I glance at each other with questions in our eyes—how are we supposed to keep a low profile, if we're staying in the full dining room, right in everybody's faces?

But when we sit down I notice the thin film of magic around us, like air burning hot in summer. Xerxes' magic, shielding our presence from the others, casting a glamour that makes it seem we're normal people. I look around. Indeed, guests move between tables laughing and talking like nothing is amiss. If they could see us clearly they'd be staring.

Lysander holds my chair, and when I sit down I meet Xerxes' gaze. His irises seem made of liquid fire. He looks as cool and unimpressed as a moment ago.

"Remove your silver magic from her," he tells Lysander, who's taken the seat by my side. "I need to feel her power in order to know she's who you say she is."

Lysander hesitates, but in the end he lowers his head, his golden hair falling over the sides of his face as he whispers the spell. I can feel it curling around me like aromatic smoke, drawing the silver markings out of my skin, and lifting them up into the air.

The low burn of power I felt in my core the entire time rises, fast and violently. I grip Lysander's hand.

"Help me," I whisper when he looks at me. "Balance me out."

He focuses, taking the extra charge from me. In a few seconds I can breathe again, enjoying the whirling power in my core, power that now feels like a purring lioness. Power that enjoys and accepts Lysander's touch.

"Fascinating," Xerxes says, and the hairs on my arms stand on end. This time his voice is spectral, demonic, giving me goose-bumps.

One thing is for sure, I can't imagine being alone with this creature. He's literally handsome as hell, but his presence is hard to bear, and his gaze and his voice even more so.

"So you really are the ocean king's descendant," he says with the ghost of a smile. My lips twitch as I try to smile back. I feel powerful magic coming from him, slipping under my dress and exploring my body to feel the nature of my magic. My skin crawls, and Lysander's fist hardens over my hand.

"Stop that," he hisses at Xerxes. "She's not yours yet."

"But she will be," the fire fae says in his disturbing voice.

"You need to take the blood oath before anything happens. And that's not the only thing I want from you."

Xerxes sits back on his chair like a boss, and places a hand on the table. It has black, sharp nails. I imagine that hand on me, and it's all I can do not to panic.

"We agreed on a mutual blood oath, and that's what I came here for. Now you want to add something to the list?"

"I'm not adding anything," Lysander counters. "I only demand to know exactly what you're going to use Arielle's powers for. And do not lie, because I want that answer tied to the blood oath, so you won't be able to change what you tell me now."

"I won't be trying to take over the Winter Realm. Isn't that enough?"

"No, because if you take over other dimensions, sooner or later the Winter Realm will fall apart under their weight. So tell me, Xerxes. What *exactly* are you going to use her power for?"

Xerxes taps the table with his sharp fingernails. Menace oozes from the hard planes of his face.

"I can't tell you now, but I'll make you a deal. I'll tell you under the blood oath. Not before."

"Under the blood oath, but *before* Arielle is bound to you forever."

"Fine." Xerxes waves his hand, relaxed.

Sandros sniffs the air, as if picking up a strange scent. Magic crackles in his hand, which means he senses a hidden threat. I immediately think of the strange magic the other fae picked up on down in the cabin, and adrenaline trickles into my veins. I assess the warriors flanking Xerxes. There's four of them, all fire fae, all men, but I'm pretty sure the threat doesn't come from them.

"All right," Lysander says. "You've seen the girl, ascertained her identity and her magic. Let's get this behind us, and make the final arrangements."

"No arrangements needed, Lysander, I'm ready for the blood oath right now."

Say what? My eyes shoot to Lysander. He won't let this happen, will he?

"It doesn't work like that, Xerxes, and you know it. We need sacred ground to make the blood bond."

"But we do have sacred ground here. They have a chapel on this ship. As long as it's sacred to the humans, we can use it, too. Why prolong this, Lysander? Let us seal the deal. How long have you been waiting for an opportunity like this to finally secure safety for all winter fae?" Xerxes grins, moving his hand like a relaxed gentleman, but the smallest muscles on his face are tense. He's hiding something. He really wants this to happen here and now, but I'm panicking too hard to think of a way to slow it down.

Lysander also seems determined not to trade me over now.

"Or maybe we should do what I originally suggested—you and me, a fight to the death."

My jaw drops.

"What the hell has gotten into you?" Sandros growls at him.

"Yeah, what the hell has gotten into you, Lysander?" Xerxes says, holding Lysander's stare.

"You worked so hard to make a deal with me, and now suddenly this?"

"I can feel the trickery behind this, Xerxes. I can smell magic I can't place, an ace you're keeping up your sleeve. You're trying to force this to go faster so you can strike with a hidden plan."

"You and I wanted to fight each other to the death long ago, but we decided it would have eventually led to more war between our people. Many would seek revenge, and chaos would reign. Now you're willing to take that risk? You're willing to risk war, your people slaughtered—" His points with his black-clawed finger. "For her?"

My eyes dart to Lysander. His hand is firmly closed on mine, his jaw set, his eyes luminous. Xerxes throws his head back, laughing, taking up space between the two fae in suits flanking him. The man seems larger than life. Lysander also grows colder, flowers of ice spreading over his skin like beautiful drawings. I can see them through his shirt. Coldness radiates from him, touching my skin, and making it pebble.

"What in the world?" I try to keep my tone down, but the coldness grows until small ice flowers appear on my own skin. I try to yank my hand from his, but he doesn't let me, probably to keep my powers in check.

My eyes fly to Xerxes. His own irises are like molten lava, watching for Lysander's next move. Both men grow tense, I can feel Lysander's muscles cord up against my arm.

"You care about her," Xerxes hisses, narrowing his eyes as he probes Lysander's stare. He leans forward, as if inspecting something interesting close up. "Tell me the truth, Ice King. Are you falling for a water nymph?"

"I'm not just a nymph." The cold Lysander emanates must be messing with my head, because I have little control over what comes out of my trembling mouth. "I am the ocean king's descendant. I have been raised in the mortal world because my aunt felt it was safer for me that way—because of people like you, King Xerxes. I know there's a great difference between the two of us, you're old and powerful, while I'm just a girl. But you lived in the supernatural world, you had an entire universe of resources at your disposal to develop your powers. While I lived in hiding in the mortal realm, barely scratching the surface of my true power. And now you're trying to rip off that power. You might be big and strong, King Xerxes, but you're a lame excuse for a man."

The lava in his eyes flares, and his black claws curl into the table, his dark lips tightening. He's terrifying with the shadows of wrath rising around him, but I'm so mad I can't stop. I provoke him even more.

"A weak man," I press onward, wanting to make him feel as hurt and humiliated as I feel. "Who needs the power of a half-fae girl?"

Xerxes looks like he's about to explode in a rage, but in the end he bursts into laughter. I lean back, surprised. Not what I expected.

"For a half-breed raised in the mortal realm you sure have a lot of nerve. But you're just a simple girl with a lucky heritage. Without that heritage and your water powers, you're not worth more than that dress you're wearing."

"Stop," Lysander growls. Ice crawls over the shimmering shield that Xerxes has created against the others, the sharp cold a menace in itself, making the fae on Xerxes' side uncomfortable.

But I keep my eyes on the molten lava in Xerxes' irises. I feel a rumble down in the floor, right under my feet. Must be the tension between the two men, but the rumbling intensifies, sending ripples through the soles of my feet. The flesh trembles up my thighs to the rest of my body.

The porcelain plates, cutlery and glass clatter against the table. We're separated from the rest of the saloon through Xerxes' shield, which is why the screams reaching my ears are muffled. But I realize with widening eyes that people run around scared, tables hitting the ground as the floor trembles so hard I'm afraid it'll break apart. I jump off the chair, my hand slipping from Lysander's grip. Edith shrieks, and Sandros pushes her behind himself, shielding her with his body.

"The strange magic that we felt," Eldan's voice rises over the noise. He's quick to draw ice from his fingertips, blades like icicles sliding out from under his sleeves.

Xerxes laughs, still relaxed in his chair, but his men jump up, facing us with shadows coiling like fumes from their bodies. We're inside the dome of

Xerxes' shield, half encrusted with ice, half embraced by shadows. The smell of burnt paper teases my nostrils, making them flare.

"God," I grunt as the itch crawls up my skin, making me scratch. "I'm allergic to smoke." I start scratching violently. I totally forgot about my allergies with all that's happened, but without my meds I'll scratch the skin off my muscles.

"If you want a deal with me, you'll have to seal it now, Lysander," Xerxes speaks in his demonic voice, everything around us shaking. "Just to be sure you won't change your mind by the next time we meet."

Lysander puts a cold arm around me, and I press myself against it. It feels like a frozen rock, and his cold embrace soothes my itching skin.

"There won't be a next time, Xerxes. You're the one who can't be trusted. You're backstabbing me as we speak."

Xerxes hisses, and one of his men throws himself at us, but Sandros slices his throat in a second with an ice dagger. Both Edith and I scream as black blood gushes out of the attacker. Lysander pushes me behind him, his big hand on my hip, pressing me to his back. My eyes roll back as I enjoy the cooling sensation of his ice covered back on my skin. I push my bare chest against him, wishing his shirt didn't exist between us. The relief is pure heaven, a mighty fucked up sensation in the hell that's going on around me.

"Give her up, Lysander."

The ship tilts, my feet skid to the side, but Lysander keeps his ground as if rooted in it. His arm is a barrier that keeps me in place. It gets hotter in here, the ice subsiding. The shadows eat more of the dome until ice starts to melt.

"You're already losing, King of Ice," Xerxes' insists in his spectral voice. "But I'll let you and your people get out of here alive, even your pets, if you leave her with me."

"I won't." I can hear in his voice that he's straining against Xerxes' shadows. "Fight me," Lysander growls. "Just you and me, and settle this once and for all."

"As much as I would love to do that, Lysander, for the sake of making it clear which one of us is the better warrior, no. I want the nymph. If having her is the only way to get her power, so be it."

The air turns so hot I can barely breathe now. I open my mouth to say something, but my throat is clogged from the smoke. Then the dome starts ripping in places like burning paper, and I get some air.

"Milord, the shield," one of the fire fae calls. I can hear the chair crack as Xerxes shoots up.

"How did you do this?" I know the words are for Lysander. The ice king is still tense, but not panicking.

"You're not the only one who brought an ace in his sleeve."

He pushes me off of him, sending me flying towards the wall. My body hurts as it disconnects from his, and I lose a sigh, my hands outstretched for him until I hit the wall, and fall to the ground.

The ship tilts violently, tables flying through the air, and through the large windows I see mighty waves rising over us. Lysander attacks Xerxes, two large fae kings crashing against each other like two meteorites. I crawl on the floor, grabbing on to a piece of iron jutting out from the metal wall. I try to connect to the ocean's power, and calm down the waves, but I'm not strong enough. I don't have access to my power.

Looking down at myself, I see a drawing like a silver bracelet around my wrist—Lysander must have quietly cast back part of the silver spell to keep my powers down when I'm disconnected from him. Despair takes me as I look out at the angry waves, screaming in frustration that I can't do anything about it.

The ship tilts hard, my body knocking into the wall, a table flying right at me. At this speed, it could knock me unconscious. But, in the last moment, a hand grabs me and pulls me to the side.

I skid behind a tilted table, Pablo holding it like a shield to protect us from flying objects.

"Grip the other side," he shrieks, his eyes wild. But it's not just fear I see in them. There's concentration, too. Edith slides by his side, grabbing a side of the table.

"We have to help Lysander," I call, desperate.

"I'm trying," Pablo says. "But the storm, it's not common fae magic, it's somehow related to Xerxes' fire core."

"What the hell are you talking about?"

He and Edith glance at each other, as if deciding to share a sensitive secret with me.

"There's a reason why they brought us along, it wasn't just to serve as your retinue—a weak pretext anyway," Pablo says. "I'm not a high fae, but I have a secret skill. I can dampen other fae's magic, if it's not their organic, main power. But Xerxes isn't using common magic to do this, like he did to create the protective dome. This is connected to his fire essence somehow, to his core powerhouse, and I can't hack that. In short, I can destroy superficial stuff, but not a fae's real essence, their being."

It dawns on me—that's why Lysander could keep his cool and his focus in the face of what Xerxes did. The fire king tried to intimidate him, but he truly had an ace up his sleeve. Or two. I look to Edith. She understands the question without me asking it.

"My family are the keepers of lore and knowledge in the Winter Realm. If there's something I don't know, I will at the very least know where and how to find it. I've done some research on how the Fire King might be destroyed, and I've brought along some theories, just in case."

So Lysander Nightfrost is more than just a power-mongering warrior who found his way to the top through violence. He's a fantastic strategist. An idea hits me, and I look to Pablo.

"The silver spell Lysander put on me. It's a spell unrelated to ice. It's magic unrelated to his core?"

He nods. Something smashes against the table, cracking it and making us all wince. We pull deeper behind it.

"Quickly, Pablo, please. Break the silver chains Lysander put on me."

"What?"

The ship tilts, making a groaning noise like the insides of a whale. I grip my side of the table tighter with one hand, showing him the silver bracelet on the other.

"I'm the descendant of the ocean. If Xerxes connected to his power somehow, I can also connect to mine. Out here at sea I should have more than him."

"But you don't know how to use it," Edith warns. "Complete command of your power could create chaos. Lysander put that bracelet on your skin to keep you safe."

"Chaos is already here, Edith, just look around. Besides, you're a keeper of knowledge. You can help me, guide me."

"It could overwhelm you before I get the chance, Arielle, these things are complicated."

"I never imagined otherwise, but what choice do we have?"

We all peek out. I can't see Lysander with Xerxes anywhere.

"Quickly, we don't have much time," I insist, panicking. I don't want anything happening to Lysander.

"Oh, fuck, okay, fine," Pablo mumbles. "Here we go." He closes his eyes slowly, breathing deeply in and out, as if calming himself down for meditation. He sinks smoothly down into his inner being like a yogi, and the silver drawing peels itself off my skin.

The ship sways harder. I catch myself against the wall, but Pablo slips. Edith catches him against her chest, whispering in his ear, and he sinks back into his trance. The silver bracelet disengages from me, rising into the air. I watch it as it loosens up into strings and disappears through the ceiling.

The more distance it takes from me the freer I feel, my eyes rolling backwards as power starts writhing in my lower belly. I close my eyes, listening to how the ocean calls for me. I can feel it deep in my body. My flesh changes consistency, and the last thing I hear in my human form is Edith whispering, "Just go with the flow." She keeps talking, but I don't listen like a human or fae anymore. Her words transform into energy that guides.

Now I'm all water, and I know where Xerxes' power comes from. I know what he's doing, how he'd played this all along. I have no more thoughts, I'm just consciousness as my body spills on the floor, becoming a pool of water searching for Lysander's magic.

I identify all the fae by their energy, and I can track them down like a dog tracks scent. I flow in a pool of waves down the stairs to the lower decks. I find the two men down in the machine room, the electronic equipment rattling and shaking.

Neither of them looks like I last saw them up on the saloon deck. Xerxes is even larger, his body glowing gold, his eyes ablaze, shadows flying from him as he throws punches at Lysander. If I still had a heart, it would jump now that I see the Lord of Winter. He's large, too, his body and his hair a sleek mixture of ice and liquid metal that allows him to move, but when Xerxes' punches land against him the fire fae's bones crack. He groans and falls back, but when Lysander's fist crashes into his ribs, his knuckles start to melt, causing him to back off, too.

They circle each other, eyes fixed, hissing like beasts made of fire and shadow, ice and metal. They spew magic rapidly, Xerxes throwing balls of fire with shadows curling around them. Lysander flashes out of their way, throwing blades of ice in return. They're both magnificent to behold, much beyond any expectations I might have had for high fae back when I was still in the mortal world, and all they really were to me was fairy tales.

I'm desperate to help Lysander, but I'm not sure how. I connect to Edith's words, letting their energy flow into me. I can feel the ocean's power rumbling inside of me, sending ripples all through my liquid body.

But when the ship rumbles and shakes again, throwing Lysander off balance, I can't wait anymore. I need to do something, and I go for the first thing I feel I can control—taking the shape of my body, but keeping the water composition; changing back into a human would probably put me through the same thing it did after the test, and I wouldn't be useful to anyone as a violently shaking wreck that curls in on itself on the floor. Unfortunately for me, shifting isn't the easy process I read about in shifter novels.

"Lysander," I call, and both men look at me. Their eyes widen as they realize who's standing in front of them, and I slowly grin at Xerxes. "Pretty good for a simple water nymph, wouldn't you say?" Probably not the smartest thing to say, but it felt good.

"It's the volcanoes on the sea bed," I tell Lysander. "There's a chain of them, and Xerxes activated them all. That's how he can draw on fire power without having actually broken the rules you set for this meeting."

Lysander glares at Xerxes, his sharp blue eyes menacing. "I should have known. You've never been more than a trickster."

"Trickster, yes, and I outsmarted you on this one." Xerxes spreads his arms, blazing like a blinding red sun, shadows fuming from him. He's gathering all his power, intensifying the eruptions. The ship groans and crackles, and I can feel the floor under me start to rip.

My only chance right now is to give in to my instincts. I basically throw myself at Lysander, my body completely made of water. He catches me out of reflex, and my arms go around his neck.

"Use the ocean power through me. It will respond to your calling, I promise you that. But you have to use me like a voodoo doll."

"No, we don't know how much you can withstand."

"This is the time to act first, and think later, Lysander."

He looks long at me, hesitating, but the ground tears.

"Do it now," I urge, "or this ship is going to break apart like the Titanic." I can feel its history in my water cells. I realize I have access to all of the ocean's knowledge, all I have to do is think about it.

Lysander cups my face that's made of water, searching it as if he's trying to see my features. "If this is the last time we see each other, I'm sorry for what I did to you, all of it. And know this—if what happens now kills you, I will let Xerxes kill me, too. I'll pay with my own blood for your life, and join you wherever you go, heaven or hell." He slits his palm with an ice claw, and blood like liquid ice swells from the cut.

He holds the cut at my mouth. "Drink it, it's a blood oath."

"No," Xerxes growls, blazing as the ship shakes, sending violent ripples through my water body.

"Do it," Lysander calls, and I grab on to his forearm, putting my lips on the cut and sucking on his blood. It flows through me like ambrosia. I even hear myself sigh, but then a blade slices through me, and my eyes snap open.

I look up into Lysander's eyes, realizing our bodies are connected through an ice blade that emerges from his hand. Parts of my body turn painfully to ice, rising like spikes. A huge thorn of ice pierces the ship wall behind Xerxes at the same time. I realize that the ocean mirrors what's happening to my body.

Xerxes roars in frustration. Another thorn breaks through the wall, then another. Lysander is turning the ocean water into blades of ice, stabbing the ship.

He's sinking it. I think of all the people aboard, but since I can sense the ocean and access information, I see that all of them are in rescue boats already, on the other side of the ship, where the ocean is still all water, and no ice. Xerxes is losing the battle and cries out in anger. His power weakens drastically as Lysander's grows.

"This isn't over yet, Lysander Nightfrost," he promises in his spectral voice that gives me the chills.

"I will have the ocean's daughter, all her power, and, before I kill you, I'll fuck her right before your eyes."

He gives out a long, powerful howl that makes me want to cover my ears, but I can't, my body being completely at Lysander's disposal. But I can see Xerxes' glow and shadows intensifying as he throws himself through the wall on the water side of the ocean, jumping in.

"I can get him," I say. My instincts have completely taken over. I rip myself from Lysander's blade, pushing myself off of him. I scream, taking my hand to what I expect to be a wound, but find nothing but water closing to reform my body perfectly.

"Arielle, no," Lysander calls, but I can't control my need to go after Xerxes. I'm so sure I can take him.

I throw myself after him, flying like an arrow into the water. I swim down after him, eyes set on the threads of fire and shadow curling upwards from his rapidly moving feet. We move so fast that I have to rocket like a bomb through a school of fish. I veer to avoid rocks and a sharp mast of a shipwreck balancing precariously between them.

I'm not afraid of anything, even though I have a deep respect for everything that surrounds me—only, it's not only surrounding me, it's all actually part of my body. I am the shark as much as I am this arrow of water plummeting after Xerxes.

He disappears into a volcano crater, lava gurgling at its top. As the liquid fire swallows him, I become wary. I don't feel the same about this volcano as I do about the rest of the sea. I pull the brakes and shoot back upwards, but the volcano erupts, and lava lands on me. I can feel Xerxes' war magic in it, and it hurts like hell. I scream, but water bubbles is all that escapes my mouth, no one can hear me. The fire tugs on me, pulling me into the crater, but at the last minute powerful hands grip me under my arms, and pull me away from the erupting lava.

We swim upwards towards the beams of light filtering through the waves, towards the rippling surface of the sea. We emerge at the surface, the sun blinding me. I draw a deep breath that burns my lungs, and I know that my body is again made of flesh.

My savior's powerful arm coils around my waist as he swims with me to the shore. My arms shake as my palms sink into something wet, and I drop facedown   into   snow.

CHAPTER VI

Arielle

I wake up in a rustic chamber. It looks like an old inn or something, judging by the wooden beams above my head. I rub my eyes, not even knowing my name yet. When I open them again to the vintage lamp on my right, hands on the sheepskin duvet, I remember what happened.

Edith and Pablo! The passengers on that ship!

I throw off the quilt and drag myself to the door, but it's locked. I pull like a lunatic, banging on it, screaming, but nothing happens. I walk to the window as quickly and as well as I can. I'm not feeling by far as bad as the first time my body shifted from water-girl to flesh-girl, but I still feel drained, exhausted, my limbs trembling as if I've been swimming for days.

Everything is white outside. Snow covers the ground, hanging heavy on trees, smoke rising from the chimneys. Down the slope there's a small square with an adorned Christmas tree.

My mind keeps spinning around Edith and Pablo, desperate for their lives. Lysander is forever present in my head, but I know for a fact that he's fine. I remember clearly how Xerxes threw himself into the water and swam to his own portal—the volcano at the bottom of the ocean—, and Xerxes was the only one who could have hurt Lysander.

The only question is now, who will find me first—Lysander or Xerxes.

The lock turns, and I spin around, a little too fast. Still not completely readjusted to my human body, I grab the wooden windowsill to steady myself. The heavy oak door opens and Lysander bends his head down to fit through the doorframe and enters, a tray of food in one hand. He stops in his tracks.

My heart swells when I lay eyes on his familiar beauty. His golden hair flows to his large shoulders, his usually cutting blue eyes staring at me full of a strange emotion. Like I'm a dear sight to him as well, but there's more. There's a strange fire in his eyes.

He shuts the door and starts towards me. I push myself against the windowsill behind me. Lysander stops, realizing that I'm wary of him. It's that fire in his gaze that unsettles me. Maybe I should ask him to say something. Maybe hearing his voice could ascertain that it's truly him.

He approaches a small wooden table in a corner, a cozy lamp flickering on it. There are only two chairs. He sets the tray on the table. Only now I start to smell the scent of butter on the steaming croissants. As my eyes wander over the eggs, the bread, the small packages of honey and chocolate, my stomach starts to grumble. My human senses are recovering. I sit down in a chair and start to tear at the food. It melts deliciously on my tongue as I lean back with my eyes closed, moaning with pleasure.

When I open them again I find Lysander sitting down across from me, too large for the chair. I swallow the bite in my mouth. This is the second time I've seen him wearing normal human clothes, this time a blue knit sweater that compliments his skin, his eyes, and definitely accents the muscular shape of his body. He leans forward on his knees, bringing his big hands together. Dark denim wraps his strong legs.

"Edith and Pablo," I say in a cracking voice, taking a hand to my throat. It hurts as if I haven't talked in a long time. "Are they all right?" I manage.

"They're resting next door."

I want to ask where we are, but my throat hurts too much.

"We're at an inn in a winter resort village in France," Lysander offers. He glances to the window. "I made sure the weather played along. It's easy in the mountains, with the heights and the wind. It will protect us from attacks, should Xerxes try something, but that shouldn't happen for a while. He doesn't know where we are, and he won't figure it out anytime soon."

"Why not?"

Lysander's beautifully contoured mouth crooks to one side in an almost sad grin. "Because the last thing he would suspect is that the law enforcer broke the law, and brought you to the mortal realm."

"What?" My hand flies back to my throat. The pain is sharp as hell.

Lysander looks me up and down with a frown, then comes up to his feet and places a hand on the nape of my neck. Current runs through me when our skin makes contact, even though I know all he's doing is assessing the state of my health.

"Every time you shift, your body puts itself back together, which is why the process is so exhausting." He pauses, eyes fixed on one point in space as he feels my body with his hand, his palm traveling down my back over what I now notice is a plain white cotton nightgown. God, I must look like shit.

"Apparently, there are also benefits to this process. It would seem you're healthier and stronger every time."

"It sure doesn't feel that way," I croak, picking up the steaming mug of tea. I take a sip, letting the hot liquid travel down to my stomach. "God, this is good."

"You seem to be taking it better than the first time, which can only mean that soon shifting will stop straining you."

"I'm not sure I want to shift again." The tea soothes my vocal cords, making it easier to talk.

Lysander sits back down in his chair, regarding me with that disturbing look in his eyes.

"What you did down there, Arielle, it was... it was magnificent."

Admiration, yes. That's one thing I see in his gaze, but it's not the *only* thing.

"I couldn't have done any of it without Pablo. And it was your idea to take him along."

Lysander smiles, still reserved, but genuinely pleased. "Yes, I had plan a plan A and a plan B, as well as a plan C to escape Xerxes if things got ugly, but nothing close to your brilliant intervention. Arielle, I'm really sorry I put you in danger, and believe that I meant it with all my heart when I said I would give you my life for it, and follow you into heaven or hell."

Blood picks up speed in my veins. The way he's saying this, it's making me feel things I don't want to feel.

"Please believe me, I was set on protecting you no matter what, and I'd planned the meeting well. I set it in the middle of the ocean especially so Xerxes wouldn't be able to use his fire powers, but he found a way to channel them anyway. But what you did, it was... He didn't stand a chance against you." He sounds proud.

"Thank you." My cheeks burn, so I look down. I don't know how to take compliments. "But I'm sure you're just saying that as a reward, to make me feel good about myself."

"I wouldn't dare to insult your intelligence like that."

His words, the soft feel of his deep voice, it's stirring feelings inside me, and cravings in my belly. I can't eat anymore, my throat closes as my heart beats faster, my chest moving a bit too fast up and down. I hope to God it doesn't betray the effect he has on me. I need to stop these feelings, choke them.

"I appreciate the compliment, Lysander, but it doesn't change anything about the fact that you wanted to trade me over to him."

"Arielle." He reaches over the table and takes my hand. I forget how to breathe as his huge fist swallows it, his knuckles as if made of ice. But his touch feels pleasantly warm on my skin. "I was willing to fight him to the death in order to prevent that from happening."

"Only because you were afraid he might prove more cunning than you, and use me in ways that you didn't anticipate. You realized on the spot that, even if he promised you peace through a blood oath, sooner or later his spreading reign of fire and chaos would swallow the Winter Realm." My eyes narrow in suspicion. "So you changed your plans. Maybe you decided you wanted my power for yourself."

His features tense up, his eyes sharpening. I grin.

"It's true, isn't it?"

"No."

"But it crossed your mind."

"If I'd wanted to keep you for myself only to misuse your power, it would have been my first option, don't you think? I would have done it in the first place."

"No, because you hadn't wasted a thought on me before you met me. While Xerxes had been actively searching for me since the day my father died. So your first idea was to trade me over, in exchange for his blood oath."

"A blood oath that I now gave to you, promising I would die with you, if I had to."

I bite my lower lip, my synapses firing like crazy. There has to be a catch in all this, and I will sure as hell bring it to light. Something's not right about the way he looks at me with those eyes of ice that yet seem to blaze.

"You're ancient, and on that ship you proved a terrific strategist. Taking Pablo with you to trick your opponents and dampen their magic, and Edith to help you with the lore, ancient knowledge, and spells. Surely the blood oath you made to me was part of your strategy."

His face sharpens with anger. He stands, his eyes fixed on my face.

"I can see that earning your trust is a losing battle, and on one hand I can understand that. I took you from the mortal realm as punishment for using your magic there, and threw you in a dungeon. Then I watched as my Council put you through a test that could have killed you, I bound your powers with my silver spells, and almost traded you over to Xerxes in exchange for a blood oath that our war would stop.

"But whether you believe me or not, what happened on that ship was real. And I am genuinely impressed by you, by what you did, by everything you represent. But some of your fears are true—I cannot afford to lose you. Yet not for the reasons you think."

He walks to the window, staring out into the winter landscape. It started to snow thick snowflakes.

"Is that why the room was locked when I woke up? Because you can't 'afford' to lose me?"

He ignores my question. "We'll be safe here for a while, until Xerxes figures out where we are," he says, hooking his thumbs into the pockets of his jeans.

"That's not an answer."

"We'll have to use the time to strengthen you, help you master your powers so you can protect yourself. With your magic unleashed, and properly controlled, he'll respect you more, and won't attack you easily."

"Good. And when I'm ready, I will have my freedom of you. You'd be doing me a great favor helping me with my powers, but you've also hurt me a lot, and I can't afford to trust you, ever. But if you mentor me, I'll consider that you've balanced the scale, and that we owe nothing more to each other."

"I'm afraid that's not going to work, Arielle."

I square my shoulders, defying him. "Are you denying me my freedom still, Lord of Winter?" I glance outside, putting two and two together. "Wait a minute, of course you are."

"With that kind of snow, nobody is getting into this town, and nobody is leaving," he confirms. "You're trapped here."

"So you're keeping me hostage again. You know what, Aunt Miriam was right. People don't change. An abuser is always an abuser, and more often than not he'll disguise himself as a kind protector."

"You and I are meant to be together, Arielle," he says in a soft, seductive voice. His eyes are intense on me. "You felt it, too, every time we touched. When I first raised your body temperature, when we were together in the water, on the ship. Our bodies work perfectly with each other, they crave each other. So do our powers."

My upper lip curls over my teeth. "I felt your blade pierce me after you swore that oath to me. It didn't feel very loving."

"You offered me your power to defeat Xerxes. It was what I needed to do, he can only be killed with ice."

"I *lent* you my power that one occasion, it doesn't mean I'm eager to share it with you again."

"Arielle, you have to understand, you need protection. Xerxes would misuse your power, the ocean witch and her people will hunt you down to kill you, and heaven knows what other supernaturals have planned for the only descendant of the ocean king. You can't be out there without the protection of someone powerful."

I tap my chin with my finger. "Now where have I heard that before? Oh, yeah, I remember. In old movies, where men teach women to fear their own power, intimidate them, make them feel they're only safe under their wing." I stand up, even though my limbs are still trembling. "But I don't fear my own power, Lysander. I might not be able to control it yet, but Edith will help. She's a keeper of knowledge, she'll be able to guide me."

"You don't know what you're up against. This isn't child's play. You need me." He walks over, and takes my hands in his big palms. Pleasure ripples over my skin, and I know he feels it, too. "The supernatural world is vaster than you can imagine, and very dangerous. You have no idea what's coming at you. But it's huge, and you're not strong enough to make your own choices."

"How convenient," I hiss. "If the half-breed doesn't do what you want, you just force her to."

"I can't let you leave and go to your death. I can't lose you." His icy eyes seem to burn as he says the words. I can feel my insides melt.

It's like the whole world started to revolve around his face, beautiful and icy. He's an angel with perfect sculpted features and lips that seem to have a magic of their own tugging at me. Wait a minute... I try to push him away.

"What the hell Lysander, are you using your magic on me?"

He doesn't let me go, his hands locking on mine. "The magic happens between us without me doing anything, and you know it. It was there from the beginning. It was there when I first drove heat into your body after the test, it was there when we crossed through the ocean portal together, and it was there on the ship, when we fought Xerxes."

I snort, fighting the emotion simmering between us. "On the day we met you tied me from neck to feet in ice thorns, and threw me in a dungeon. You would have left me there to die. You didn't give a shit about the magic between us then."

"You have to understand, keeping the secret of the supernatural realms from humans is of utmost importance. Drastically punishing offenders has been the only successful strategy to make sure it doesn't happen a lot."

"So you have always ruled with fear."

"All high fae do, because it's effective."

"It would be effective for humans, too, but still catastrophic."

"It's different for fae. They're far stronger than humans, not to mention they're far older. They take things differently."

I raise my chin.

"I will not share my power with you, Lysander. It's mine alone, and I intend to keep it. And I won't be traded to Xerxes in order to end the war between fire and ice either, and you know why? Because you're right, sooner or later it'll break out again. Maybe not in a year, or two, or a thousand, but one day, Xerxes will fall, and so will you. And your successors won't have a reason to honor your blood bond, even if you do make one in the end."

"Xerxes won't fall anytime soon. And I won't either."

"Still, neither of you can truly guarantee this peace will last forever."

"Think about your Aunt Miriam." His voice is lower, like he didn't want to go there, but he's forced to. I scoff.

"Finally you show your true face. You'd do anything to get your hands on my power, wouldn't you, even pretend to be—" My heart jolts at the idea, but I push it back down. "Falling in love with me."

I yank my hands away from him, and he lets me go this time. I can barely keep from slapping him, so I walk briskly to the window. I stare outside at the fairy tale winter, big snowflakes landing on the windowpane.

"You come in here acting all 'we're meant to be together', and yet once again you keep me in a prison, and threaten me in order to force my cooperation. So no, Lysander. My answer is no. And if you choose to harm Aunt Miriam, I'll find a way to get to Xerxes myself, and lay my powers at his feet. That will be my revenge."

"Fine," he says. "You leave me no choice."

His words are full of hurt, but they're also like a spell, I can feel the magic in them. I think he's trying to manipulate my mood again, but then I feel his magic trickling over my skin, and I realize what's happening.

"What, no!" I shriek, looking down at my arms as the silver drawings spread over them, sinking in until all that remains are faint traces. Now if I try to use my powers, silver chains will glow and keep them down.

I turn angrily and charge at Lysander, smashing my fists against his chest. "You bastard."

He lets me beat his chest, not even trying to block me. He just takes it, watching me as tears stream down my face.

"You have no right to rip it away from me, absolutely no right!"

"It's doing nothing for you but put you in danger. And if you won't work with me, for your own protection, I have no other way to ensure your safety."

"You're not protecting me, you're punishing me!"

"You seem bent on thinking the worst of me, and you won't let anything change that. I respect your choice, and I even understand it, to a certain extent. But I will still do everything in my power to protect you, Arielle, even if it means chaining you again, and earning myself your deepest hatred. Oh, and don't even think of having Pablo lift the spell, because this time the magic is much more powerful than the first time, and it's tied to my ice core. Also, it's tied to my life. That means the spell will only lift if I do it, or if I die. Anyone who tries to lift it, no matter how

133

powerful, will die trying. This applies to the ocean witch, too, maybe even Xerxes."

I've stopped hitting him, my eyes widening with every word as I realize what he's done.

"You may hate me," he continues, "but at least I know you'll be a hundred percent safe. No one can lift your magic without dying. And neither can they kill you, because if you die, your power is lost forever, which is to nobody's advantage." He turns on his heel, and heads for the door, where he stops one last time. "One day you'll thank me for this."

He exits without looking back, but only a moment later Edith and Pablo appear in the doorway, eyes darting from the leaving Lysander to me. The moment I lock eyes with my friend Edith I drop to my knees, and release all of the pent up anger in loud sobs, my face hidden in my palms.

"Arielle." Edith and Pablo run to me, but I can't stop crying, releasing all the powerlessness and the grief. A feeling of loss takes over me, now that the whirl of power in my lower belly has stilled down to a barely noticeable whir.

"He'll pay for this," I mumble, "I swear to God he'll pay for this."

Arielle

"I DO BELIEVE HE'S DOING it for your protection," Edith says, focused on painting my toenails. I've already done hers, and now I'm having a hot jasmine tea by the window.

"I guess. But mainly he's doing it for his own agenda. Have you seen him lately, by the way?"

She shrugs, focused on her work. "No, but I suppose we'll see him later this evening. It's Christmas Eve, after all."

"Christmas Eve," I whisper, looking out the window at the white landscape, dunes of snow glistening in the moonlight. Thick fir trees flank the slope that winds down to the village, their branches adorned with snow.

"It's like in fairy tales," I say with a smile, resting my head against the window frame, the steaming tea teasing my nostrils.

"You should see Winter Realm," she says, now looking out dreamily. "It's like this everywhere. Not only fairy tale villages like this one, but entire cities of ice, with crystal castles, sleepy towns and vibrant metropolises."

"Tell me more about it, your home. Help me picture it."

"Well, to begin with, in order to picture the map of it, you should know how the realms work. Do you?"

"I have a general idea. Aunt Miriam said that realms are actually versions of our universe. Something like parallel universes, only that they are layered, and interconnected. The middle realm is the mortal one, the least magical, in a sense, but also the main piece. So everything kind of revolves around it, which is why supernaturals guard it with so much care. Also why some darker supernaturals cross over and try to take over control. Whoever rules the Earth, tips the balance in their favor."

"Good so far. Maybe now that you think about it, you can understand why the king is so strict with the rules on crossing over and never using magic in the mortal world."

I grimace, but I see her point.

"It's true," she says, heading over to the wardrobe for our outfits. "The Winter Realm is basically a universe in which the Earth is a fairy tale winter world, but full of dangerous magic. It's a tough place, but also the most beautiful I've ever seen. I would take it over the Summer Realm anytime."

"I think I would, too. I've always loved winter."

She swirls around, holding her dress close to her chest. An idea seems to have hit her, one that makes her feel enthusiastic. "Maybe you always loved winter because deep down you sensed that you were fated to live out a love story with the Lord of Winter."

"Say what? Love story?"

"Don't pretend you don't feel anything for him, Arielle. He is the Lord of Winter and Daylight, as you are the Queen of Water and the Moon. Just think about it. You were meant to be together, you'd be indestructible as a team, and your bodies, as well as your powers feel that. Everybody around you feels it, when we see you together, we can feel the static sizzle."

I spring up from the chair, my fists balling by my sides. "Did he put you up to this?" I scan her up and down, with her long silver hair and those innocent brown eyes. "You're a winter fae, you're his subject. You have to do what he tells you. Are you trying to persuade me to give him my powers?"

Her gaze becomes harder, her tone stern. "Arielle you're losing it, you're seeing enemies everywhere.

The King has been gone since the day he talked to you in this room, and you know what? He's probably somewhere making sure you're safe, and you don't even appreciate it. He protects you even though he knows you hate him, putting himself and his entire realm at risk. That is an entire planet, Arielle, so that you fully understand. He is the king of an entire Earth, all the supernaturals in it depending on him. And you don't even try to understand his point of view."

She stares hard into my face, making it impossible to ignore her perspective. I nod, placing the tea mug on the windowsill.

"I might have gotten carried away. I understand that. But try to put yourself in my shoes. If he'd taken you from your world, chained you in ice and thrown you in a dungeon, only to take you out of it to use you, what would you feel? Especially when at the end he comes and proposes that you yield your powers to him?"

"All I know is that he's feeling genuinely protective of you. The way he pulled back from that deal with Xerxes on the ship, how he risked everything for you, he's redeemed himself in my eyes."

"He chained my powers again, Edith," I stress.

"In order to protect you! You'd probably have caused Tsunamis here, in the mortal world, by now. Let me remind you that you have very poor control over your powers. The only other way to keep them in check would have been to unite them with his."

It hits me. "Wait a minute." I walk closer to her, my feet sinking in the soft rug. "Uniting our powers would mean... Was he asking me to sleep with him?"

The fire in his eyes returns to my mind. Was he thinking about...sex?

"I don't know exactly what you talked about, but I suppose yes."

Scenarios start to spin in my head. What was Lysander actually asking me? Did he want a relationship, an affair, or something else?

"Here's what I suggest," Edith says, going back to the wardrobe and sliding clothes off the hangers. "Let's go down to the inn saloon, and have some spiced wine. I expect the king will come tonight. After a few hot mugs you'll be relaxed enough to talk to him normally. Ask him to make it clear what exactly he proposes."

She holds out a white wool dress that covers me from neck to the middle of my thighs. I look at myself in the mirror, Edith popping by my side, squeezing my shoulders. Her momentary animosity against me seems to have subsided.

"You look dashing, doll."

I think about how Lysander might have been propositioning me for sex, and I blush so hard that I can feel it reach the top of my ears.

"If you're lucky," Edith says, "he will try to persuade you again. Really now, why don't you agree to it? You're into him, that much is obvious. Would it really be so bad, giving him your virginity? He does offer protection, and you'll be able to use his powers in the same measure he'll be using yours."

I turn around briskly. "What?"

138

Edith smiles. "What did you expect, Arielle? There is no borrowing someone's power without giving them yours. It's a give and take."

Oh. My. God. "I... I didn't know that. Why didn't Lysander tell me, why didn't he use this to convince me?"

Edith places soft hands on mine. "I think he wanted the decision to come from your heart. He craves you, but he wants it to be real. He wants you to want   him   back."

139

CHAPTER VII

Lysander

I'm taking a mug of wine to my lips when I smell Arielle's scent, the scent of sea breeze and roses. I'm drawn to it like a dog to a bone. Damn it, no woman has ever had this effect on me. I watch her come down the wooden stairs with Edith, and I don't know how to react. My entire being is aware of her presence. I hoped the days I spent away from her would help, but they didn't. At all.

I down the wine and slam the mug on the counter, making the innkeeper wince. He's a big guy with a big beard and tattoos coiling over his fleshy arms, but he's been tip-toeing his way around me.

"Another, please." I push the mug across the counter. He takes it for a refill.

"In my experience," he says in his English with heavy French accent, "when a guy starts out like this, he ends up brawling and kicking my furniture." He glances at Arielle. "Especially when the main issue is a lady. And when their muscles bulge out like that." He raises his thick eyebrows at my bicep that threatens to tear the sweater. There were few stores open when I returned from the Winter Realm earlier today, since it's Christmas Eve, so my choices of clothing were limited.

The innkeeper puts his tattooed elbow on the counter, leaning towards me with a secretive air. "Come on, what stands in the way of a guy like you? There's not a woman in this room who's not been eyeing you, you could have any one you want. What stops you from banging this girl tonight?"

My eyes snap up at him, ice spreading in my irises. He steps back, bumping against the liquor shelves behind him. "Relax mate, I didn't mean to offend you. Or her."

"I'm not paying you to ask questions, especially not that kind."

My eyes sweep over the inn, now full of villagers gathered at wooden tables, a richly adorned Christmas tree by the fireplace, with presents that they can buy. Many are already playing the game of throwing a special kind of dice with numbers, and then buying the present with the number they get, for the person they choose. That way everybody gets a surprise. In the end, they can bargain among each other and exchange their presents for others. Joyful Christmas music pours from the loudspeakers, but a live band is also preparing for a show on an improvised stage under the stairs.

I see Arielle and Edith giggling. They're looking at me, both of them. They're talking about me, I can tell, and my heart reacts. I've experienced so many new emotions ever since I met Arielle de Saelaria, and I don't know how to deal with them anymore.

Edith arranges her dress, squares her shoulders and starts towards me. I expect she has something to say, but when she approaches the counter she addresses the innkeeper.

"Two mugs of spiced wine, please, with extra cinnamon."

I keep my eyes on her, my way of inviting her to talk. She clears her throat, her cheeks red. Poor thing is embarrassed.

"Milord, permission to tackle a sensitive issue of a personal nature with you."

I cock an eyebrow and raise my chin, which makes her shrink a bit. "Go ahead."

She clears her throat again. "Arielle thinks she might have got you wrong the last time you talked. So, if you like, she's willing to discuss your initial proposition again."

My eyes fly over to Arielle, who's standing in a corner in the rapidly filling room. The door opens, and more people flood in, stomping their feet against the threshold to get the snow off their boots. Others spread their arms, greeting them warmly and loudly. Arielle leans with her back against the wooden wall by the door, her cheeks red, her arms crossed over her chest, right under the round swell of her breasts.

My mouth waters as I look at her, the forbidden fruit in a white wool dress that hugs the alluring curves of her body.

I lick my lips, my eyes fixed on her. I couldn't stay away even if I wanted to, drawn to my forbidden desire like a moth to a flame. She looks at me out of those dreamy eyes, hooded by her long black eyelashes. Edith keeps talking to me, but I'm not listening anymore. I pick up one of the two mugs the innkeeper has provided, as well as my own, and head over to Arielle.

I'm so fixated on her that the entire environment fades into the background. Not that I don't feel the many pairs of eyes watching us. After all, we're fae, and we look different than humans, we appear painfully beautiful to their eyes.

As Arielle appears to me now, as I stop in front of her, and hand her a mug.

"Edith ordered this for you."

"Thank you." She takes it, holding my gaze. Her cheeks are stained crimson, her lips blood red, and I can hear her heart beating fast. Adrenaline courses through both our veins. I put a hand on the wall next to her head, blocking her in. It makes me feel that I have her full attention, which I'm so hungry for.

"What do you feel for me, Arielle?" It's like some demon has taken possession of my heart, driving my behavior, making me act like a lunatic. All the ice in the world couldn't cool these feelings down.

"I... I told you, I..." She looks down to her mug, searching for words, searching her soul. I'm afraid of what she'll find, and I lift her chin with a finger.

"Tell me it's not all bad."

"I think I understand now what you were asking me a few days ago."

"You do?"

"Maybe if you would ask me again, more directly..." Her voice fades, and she clears her throat. "Maybe my answer would be different."

If my blood were hot and red as hers, my whole face would be on fire. But my blood is like liquid ice, which helps hide my feelings. On the inside, I'm combusting.

If I speak clearly, she'd probably agree to be mine. But now things are different, and I can't do that to her. I can't make promises I can't keep, not after what I've done in the Winter Realm. I had to make a tough choice to ensure her safety forever, even if that meant losing every chance of ever having her. I thought she'd never want me, I thought I had nothing more to lose.

"I would ask you, Arielle. My feelings haven't changed. But..."

"But what?" Her voice turns seductive. The live band is striking the first notes, night has fallen over the village, and the wine is going to people's heads. I'm resilient to alcohol, but her presence, her scent of sea breeze and roses, it makes me feel drunk with growing lust.

"I cannot offer the same terms as a few days ago."

"Then maybe we can negotiate new terms." She sips her wine, giving me what I think are bedroom eyes. I can't take my eyes off of her, which I know sends signals that I shouldn't send.

"Arielle, I have ensured your safety, and that of your Aunt Miriam. If everything goes well, I might even be able to lift the chains off your sea power soon enough. You wanted to be completely free, and I've done everything in my power to ensure that for you. So you don't have to do this anymore, you don't have to offer yourself to me."

She takes another long sip of the wine, then places the empty mug on the floor. She's clearly tipsy, half from the wine she had on an empty stomach, half from the adrenaline that our exchange injects into her bloodstream. She takes my hand, drawing closer to me, and starts moving her body to the music.

My eyes slide down to her swaying hips, and my cock reacts.

"By the cursed realms," I growl under my breath.

"Dance with me, Lysander," she says seductively. The luring nymph is in her blood, and no chaining magic in the world can keep it down. We move along with the crowd, her breasts pushing against my body, right under my chest. I squeeze my eyes shut, struggling to keep down the need that courses through me.

If I give in to this attraction, no matter how maddening, it will mean deceiving Arielle once again. I can feel to the icy marrow of my bones that she will never forgive me for it, and I start to pull away.

⚬≪≫⚬

Arielle

I MUST HAVE GOTTEN him wrong. He's pulling away, pushing my hands off of him. I only get to feel those bulging muscles for a few seconds.

"Arielle, no," he drawls.

I'm a virgin with no experience, but there's no mistaking that low purr in his voice. I'm making him horny, but he's choosing to reject me. No, I've come too far, the connection between us is too strong now, and standing down would hurt, even physically.

"I'll do it, Lysander, I'll merge my power with yours."

"What made you change your mind?"

"Realizing that you had much more to think about than just me. You have an entire world to protect, to care for, as king of the Winter Realm. Plus, Edith told me the sharing of power would be mutual." I know that sounds like I'm the one mongering for his magic now, but I hope he knows that's not true.

"It means a lot to me that you have started to see things differently, Arielle." He winds an arm around my waist, pulling me close and pressing me against his rock-hard body. My power whirls inside of me, wanting to feel his, connect to it. "Please remember these words. I will protect you forever, no matter the cost. I made a blood oath that I will die with you, because I felt in my blood that I wanted to. I will always make the choices that are in your best interest. But I cannot be with you..." He looks down at our bodies that are pressed together. "This way."

But I just can't take no for an answer, not at this point. A maddening attraction tugs on me, making me stick to him like glue. I need to be with him, and I feel it deeply. He tries to move away from me, but my hand drops, and I cup his penis through the denim. He stiffens and hisses, while I lose a sigh.

I can't hold back an, "Oh God, you're huge." I bite my lower lip, looking down at the jeans molding the thick shape of his cock.

"I want you to be the first man in my life, Lysander," I say truthfully, my cheeks hot as I stare up at him again. I forgot all about shame.

"Arielle, please, stop."

But I just can't accept the distance he wants to put between us. The need for him twists and turns in my lower belly, and my fingers claw into his sweater, my fingernails tearing through it. He groans, and people hear, some turning around. But I won't pull away, I'm on fire for him. I could wind my legs around his hips and fuck him right here, on the improvised dance floor of this rustic inn.

"I need you inside of me, Lysander. I feel it so deeply that it hurts. It's a hunger I can't explain, except through the connection that has existed between us from the beginning." Edith's explanation comes to mind—he's the Lord of Ice, and I'm the Lady of Water, two elements that, united, could rule the universe. Our bodies are basically made of these elements that are dying to be together, and form an unbreakable bond. Xerxes' fire wouldn't stand a chance against Lysander and me united.

I raise my chin as our bodies sway along with the music, inviting him to kiss me. He lowers his head and finally, those sensual but powerfully contoured lips touch mine. He's gentle at first, savoring the first brush of our mouths against each other, but a moment later his arms lock around me, his mouth crashing down on mine.

"By the cursed realms," he whispers hungrily against my lips. "You are the ultimate seductress. No man could ever resist you."

He kisses me hard, his lips parting mine, his tongue flicking inside my mouth, eager to taste me. The whole world has faded in the background, even though as half-fae I'm always aware of my surroundings to spot possible threats. Here, there are none, except for the curious eyes that I can feel plastered to us. But who can blame these people? We're kissing each other like mad in the middle of a crowded room, at a Christmas party.

A dirty idea seeps into my mind. I manage to pull away from our kiss just enough to whisper, "Follow me."

He releases me from his embrace, even though it seems to hurt him. I take his hand, and lead him to the stairs. We pass Edith and Sandros on our way, the first one winking, the latter staring like he can't believe it.

I lead him up to my room, and close the door, which is enough to muffle the party sounds. My heart beats in my throat as I watch the great King Lysander Nightfrost turn to face me. Slowly, hyper-aware of my every move, I light three candles on the vanity table, the flames casting a golden glow over the rustic wooden room.

I remember the first time Lysander and I met. Also at a party, at the fraternity house, him standing in the middle of a crowded room. Too tall and too large for a human, his golden hair spilling to his shoulders, he's a delicious sight. Seeing him dressed in the clothes of a mortal, with the blue sweater hugging his strong body, I cream between my legs.

"I want to do dirty things with you, Lysander," I say, my voice charged with invitation.

"Arielle, you need to think this through," he blocks, holding his big hands up. "You're a virgin, and your first time, it should be special."

"My first time should be with you, tonight." I prance over to him, kicking off my shoes, bathing in the intimate glow of the candles. All that stands between us now is this dress, and the black lace stockings that I'm wearing. "I feel a deep longing, Lysander, as if it's not even my own decision, but a command from deep within. My entire body is screaming that you're the one."

His features harden as he keeps fighting his own cravings, but I'll be damned if I let him win.

"First there's something you should know," he says. "Something that might change your mind."

"Nothing can change my mind, because this isn't a decision I'm making with my head." I fall slowly down to my knees, and start working on his belt and his fly. He tries to pull me up, shocked, but I hook my fingers in his waistband.

I use my natural water nymph powers to help him loosen up, and lose himself in my gaze until I free his huge erection. My heart rate speeds up as I stare at it, a thick cock so hard for me the veins show. God, I'm so hungry for him that I reach with one hand inside his jeans, cupping his balls, while I hold his cock with the other and lick him from root to head.

"By the cursed realms," he growls, his thighs flexing through the denim. He cups my face with both hands, looking down at me with the need of a beast.

"I want to suck you off, Milord." I stress the last word, and his enormous cock strains against my hand that's wrapped around it. I don't know what I'm doing, but I'm doing it with heart. I wrap my lips around his large crest, and slide down to take in as much as I can of his length, sheathing my teeth.

I don't manage much, but it's enough to make him groan deeply, his hands cupping the nape of my neck.

"Oh, God, this feels so good," he rumbles.

"I aim to please, Milord."

He tries to lift me up, but I slide my mouth down his cock again, sucking hard. I know that it's driving him insane, I can feel it. It hits me that my first sexual encounter is giving a man a blowjob, and I can't believe how much I'm loving it. I even technically begged him for it.

His cock throbs in my mouth, even though I'm not even close to taking it all in. I sweat and tremble with the anticipation of this fae king's seed pouring down my throat, but he lifts me up, twirls me through the air, and falls with me on the bed.

"You're going to be the death of me," he rumbles, and tears the wool dress off of me. It happens so fast that I gasp, looking down at myself, now only in my black bra, panties, and the lace stockings. My body glows in the candlelight as Lysander's hands glide down my stomach and my legs, groaning with pleasure at what he's seeing.

"I'd like to see you naked, Milord," I whisper. "Please."

He throws off his sweater, and loses his pants as quickly as he relieved me of my dress. He crawls on the bed over me, setting my whole body on fire as I watch him. His muscles cord up under his snow-white skin, his golden hair falling over the sides of his face, brushing my neck as he puts his lips on mine.

He kisses me sweetly, but full of lust, his tongue sliding between my lips to claim my mouth. I writhe under him, my hands wandering all over his body, my fingers splayed to allow my palms to feel every muscle. But Lysander grabs my wrists, and holds them up above my head. He can't keep them there for long though, hungry to kiss my neck, and down my chest, scooping my breasts out of my bra.

I moan and writhe, opening my legs for him.

"Take me, take me now," I plead. "Fuck me."

He growls like a beast, and rips off my panties and my stockings. All I'm wearing now is my bra, my breasts out of it. He spans what's left of my stockings like a whip between his hands, and restrains by wrists above my head, tying them to the headboard.

"Please, Milord, I want to touch you."

"If you keep touching me, I'll stain you with my seed in minutes, and tomorrow you'll hate me for it."

I frown. "Why would I hate you?"

But he doesn't waste another second. He goes down on me, his tongue swiping between the folds of my pussy.

"Oh, Milord," I cry, arching my hips into his mouth as he licks me. He seems to love it when I call him that. He grabs my ass with both hands that are so huge my butt cheeks fit entirely in them, and laps at my pussy like a thirsty man in the desert.

I'm close to orgasm in no time, my breath shallow, my body writhing into his mouth. But he slows down, running a thick finger through my cream, and teasing my entrance.

"God, please Milord, let me come," I plead.

"I will, Milady," he says, his breath hot on my aching pussy. I lift my head and look at him, a mighty king between my legs, enjoying the best view possible of the most intimate part of my body. I feel so naked and vulnerable it goes beyond the physical. "But when you come, it will be a shattering orgasm that you'll never forget."

There's a sadness in the way he says it. It sounds almost like goodbye, it's gut-wrenching. He presses his sensual mouth to my pussy, his lips on my folds, and his tongue on my clit, kissing me with passion. He pushes his finger just a little bit inside me, enough to make me feel full, possessed, taken.

My head spins with pleasure, my hands straining against the tie he improvised of my stockings. I lift my hips, thrusting to meet his mouth and his fingers, so creamed that my inner thighs are wet. Climax builds up, and I finally explode in waves of pleasure on Lysander's face, screaming, my toes curling.

A guy next door bangs on the wall, calling, "That's it, do her hard, bro." It should anger me, but instead, it adds to the pleasure. I wish Lysander would thrust his cock inside me, now that I'm so wet I could surely take his whole girth. I want him to fuck me hard, the headboard banging against the wall, showing that smartass next door what real fucking sounds like.

"By the cursed realms, I love seeing you come undone," Lysander says, crawling over me and untying my wrists. I massage them gently, since I've strained so hard against them that the laced stockings reddened my skin. He scoops me in his arms, but I roll over him, taking him by surprise.

I trace the sharp warrior features of his face with my fingers, not even trying to refrain from worshipping him, which is what I feel.

"My heart is so full of you, Milord," I whisper, my eyes roaming over his face that glows beautifully in the candlelight. I kiss him, tasting myself on his lips, teasing his mouth with my tongue to let me deepen the kiss. But he places a hand on my jaw, his thumb brushing my chin. I notice that his expression has changed from one of arousal to one of sadness.

"I wish you knew how much it means to me," he says, "that you allowed me the privilege of giving you your first orgasm."

"And what an orgasm," I say, my heart bursting with emotion. "Shattering, unforgettable. And you'll give me many more, in the future."

I kiss him lightly on the lips, then go down to his neck and his rock hard chest.

"Arielle..."

I close my eyes and connect to him on that deep level only the two of us know, using the bond between us, and enjoying the feel of his body on my lips. His skin tastes of snow and ice, but it feels hot as if he has a fever.

I go down on him, taking his cock into my mouth and sliding right down to the root, hand on his balls. He growls and pushes himself into my mouth, though he says, "No, Arielle, please don't."

I suck hard, with passion and determination. I'm bent on giving him an orgasm, hoping that my being mindlessly in love with him will give me enough skill to offer him the best blowjob of his life. He finally loses it. He puts a large hand on my head, pushing me down to take him all in, finally doing what I want him to do—fuck my mouth like a Lord.

He comes inside my mouth, punching the headboard with such fury that it splinters to pieces. His seed pours down my throat, but at this point I'm shocked. I come slowly up in a sitting position, leaning back on my heels and wiping my mouth with my hand. I'm confused, and I feel a little like a street whore, seeing the violent reaction he had at the orgasm I gave him.

"What the hell have I done to make you punch the headboard like that?"

"I shouldn't have done this. I shouldn't have climaxed, now I've stained you with my seed."

"Stained me? Lysander, you and I belong together."

"No, we don't." His words rip through my heart.

"What do you mean? We've just made love to each other, for Christ's sake."

"Arielle, I had to do something when I went to the Winter Realm, something that changed things between us. I had to make deals, negotiate military support, deal with Xerxes' fire fae increased attacks on our people. All hell was breaking loose, I had to take extreme measures, and I had to do it fast."

"I totally understand, and we'll fight this together, I'm with you body and soul. With our powers united—"

"No, you don't understand. We cannot unite our powers anymore. We cannot be together, ever."

I look around confused, my eyes sweeping over the candles, and the twisted sheets on the bed that stand proof of our wild passion. "But... we made love."

"And it was great, but it can't happen again." His icy eyes stare so hard at me that it hurts. "Arielle, I had to pledge myself to marry Minerva."

TO BE CONTINUED

BOOK TWO, **KING OF FROST**, IS SCHEDULED FOR RELEASE IN JANUARY 2020. STAY TUNED BY FOLLOWING ANA CALIN ON AMAZON, OR CHECK OUT MORE AT

ANA CALIN COMPLETE WORKS

Made in the USA
Monee, IL
04 June 2022